T0061629

THE
QUEEN OF
SPADES
AND SELECTED WORKS

THE QUEEN OF SPADES

AND SELECTED WORKS

ALEXANDER PUSHKIN

TRANSLATED FROM THE RUSSIAN
BY ANTHONY BRIGGS

PUSHKIN PRESS CLASSICS

Pushkin Press
Somerset House, Strand
London WC2R 1LA

The Queen of Spades (*Pikovaya dama*) originally
published in Russian in 1834

The Stationmaster (*Stantsionnyy smotritel*) originally
published in Russian in *The Tales of the Late Ivan Petrovich
Belkin* (*Povesti pokoynogo Ivana Petrovicha Belkina*) in 1830

First published by Pushkin Press in 2012
This edition published 2024

1 3 5 7 9 8 6 4 2

ISBN 13: 978-1-80533-093-6

Designed and typeset by Tetragon, London
Printed and bound in the United Kingdom by Clays Ltd, Elcograf S.p.A.

www.pushkinpress.com

PUSHKIN PRESS CLASSICS

THE
QUEEN OF
SPADES
AND SELECTED WORKS

'An unusual selection of a surprisingly
modern master's work… worth
turning to again and again'
GUARDIAN

'Exceptionally original, elegant and
often subversively critical in his writings,
Pushkin touched depths of feeling while
cultivating an insouciant lightness'
IAIN BAMFORTH

'Charming… an ideal introduction to the man
widely regarded as the greatest Russian writer'
RUSSIA NOW

ALEXANDER PUSHKIN (1799–1837) published his first poem when he was 15, and in 1820 his first long poem—*Ruslan and Lyudmila*—brought him fame. His work, including the novel-in-verse *Yevgeny Onegin*, the poem *The Bronze Horseman*, the play *Boris Godunov* and the short story *The Queen of Spades* has secured his place as one of the greatest writers, in any language, ever to have lived. He died aged 37, having been wounded in a duel—Pushkin's 29th—by his brother-in-law.

ANTHONY BRIGGS is one of the world's leading authorities on the works of Pushkin. He is the author of *Alexander Pushkin: A Critical Study* and editor of *Alexander Pushkin: A Celebration of Russia's Best-Loved Writer*. He is also an acclaimed translator from Russian, whose translations include Tolstoy's *War and Peace*, *The Death of Ivan Ilyich* and *Resurrection*. He was shortlisted for the Rossica Translation Prize for this translation.

CONTENTS

INTRODUCTION

Alexander Pushkin (1799–1837)

Pushkin—the most subcutaneous of Russian presences.

Alexander Zholkovsky

Alexander Pushkin is one of those rare writers—like Shakespeare and Dante—whose name embodies an entire national culture. He was the creator of the modern Russian language, and the founder of his country's great literary tradition.

Born of ancient lineage on both sides of the family, and especially proud of the Abyssinian blood inherited from his great-grandfather, Pushkin received an excellent education but then went on to lead a restless and largely unhappy life. He was exiled for long periods, beset with money problems and, although famous for a time as the country's first poet, worried about his declining popularity when the vogue for poetry began to wane. Marriage, at the age of thirty-one, brought him little contentment, exacerbating many of his problems, and it was in a duel over his wife's honour that he died at the age of thirty-seven.

He was a prolific writer, the author of eight hundred lyric and a dozen narrative poems (culminating in *The Bronze Horseman*), a novel in verse (*Yevgeny Onegin*), several dramatic works (including *Boris Godunov*), a number of prose stories (including *The Queen of Spades*), and a large body of critical articles, historical studies and letters.

Pushkin did for the Russian language what Chaucer did for English—but with a big difference. Pushkin's Russian is totally of today. He created a vibrant, modern language out of several different strands that needed to be woven together, predominantly vernacular Russian, French and Old Church Slavonic. This new form of Russian he used with a sensitivity that has never been surpassed. The acoustical skill of his verse is matched with an elegant literary manner, great powers of originality and imagination, and a sophisticated style. Melodious, agreeable and playful, yet also at times disturbingly profound and serious-minded, his works are often compared to those of Mozart.

Shakespeare aside, it is doubtful whether any writer has inspired more music than Pushkin. Well over a thousand composers have set his writing to music, using hundreds of his works; songs on Pushkin's texts run into the thousands, and among our most famous operas are Tchaikovsky's *Yevgeny Onegin* and *The Queen of Spades*, and Mussorgsky's *Boris Godunov*.

Pushkin was an instinctive assimilator of the world's greatest writing. Widely read from childhood in classical and European literature, he developed the most discriminating taste and knew how to absorb and imitate without sacrificing originality. He came to match Byron for light-hearted fluency, but wrote with greater discipline and elegance. From Scott he borrowed the broad sweep of characterization which blended real historical figures with fictional men and women. Most of all, he admired Shakespeare as a master of psychological insight and consistency.

Conversely, Pushkin has had a profound effect on all subsequent Russian writers, including the greatest—Gogol, Turgenev, Dostoevsky and Tolstoy—and it continues to this day. These artists often expressed their gratitude for the gift of a great literary language, and for innumerable models to be followed, explored and developed in new works that have themselves become world-famous.

Today in Russia Pushkin remains a household name, the best-loved of all her writers. Almost all Russians know bits of Pushkin by heart, and many people have committed hundreds of his lines to memory. He provides a quotation for every family occasion and for moments of national triumph and disaster.

This man's statue, unveiled in 1880, stands proudly in what is today Moscow's Pushkin Square. In 1990, only a few hundred yards away, the first Russian fast-food outlet was opened: the Moscow McDonald's. Thus, old Russia, with its great achievements in high culture, has been set

11

against the materialist modern world, with her own future still uncertain. So far, the coalition of old and new has worked with no small degree of success. But whatever happens to that country, when the Russians need a symbolic figure to rally round they will turn not to Tolstoy, Dostoevsky or Chekhov, but to Alexander Pushkin.

Although Pushkin is remembered at home mainly for his poetry, the easiest approach for foreigners may be through his prose works. Of these, *The Queen of Spades* stands out as a masterpiece. In a story of mental collapse, the hero, Hermann, begins as a prudent onlooker at the gambling table, fascinated by the twists and turns of the cards, but ends up in an asylum. The story of how he got there is told succinctly and with forensic clarity. What could have been a tale of Gothic melodrama becomes a fascinating study in psychology, the supernatural details appearing as emanations from a sick mind.

The Stationmaster is set mainly in a remote postal station. The beautiful young daughter of the master, having charmed every visitor, including the narrator and us, suddenly disappears. Has she run away, been abducted, or worse? As the tale unfolds, in a narrative overflowing with sympathy, it builds up unforgettable portraits of the master, the girl and one traveller, on whom the outcome depends.

Pushkin's tribute to his beloved Shakespeare, *Boris Godunov*, a historical drama in blank verse, contains memorable individual scenes; we have included one famous passage, a dignified monologue, slowly declaimed by an old monk completing his record of Russian history.

Of Pushkin's four *Little Tragedies*—character-studies in blank verse—the most famous is *Mozart and Salieri*, in which Pushkin gives dramatic form to a rumour that the latter composer had poisoned the former out of jealousy. This myth has now become entrenched because of Peter Shaffer's English play *Amadeus*, which drew extensively on Pushkin, and the deserved success of the film adaptation of the same name.

There are twelve completed narrative poems, the best of which is *The Bronze Horseman*, one of the brightest gems in all Russian literature, resplendent with incident, character and ideas. It describes the building of St Petersburg in 1703, and then the sad fate of one of its poorer citizens, Yevgeny, whose dreams of domestic happiness are shattered by the real-life floods of 1824. Yevgeny's tragedy is set in a broad context, conveying the political need for a ruler to build such a city, and the indomitable power of nature. Woe betide any individual who stands in the path of historical necessity or thinks he has been spared by the surrounding elements.

The poem that follows is Pushkin's naughtiest work. Cast in the form of a folk narrative in verse, *Tsar Nikita and His Forty Daughters* tells of a sad situation. All the daughters of the Tsar (born of several wives) suffer from the same embarrassing condition; the narrator blushes to inform

13

us that they lack the one physical feature that, er, defines their femininity. Somehow a supply of these objects must be found to put things right. The story of how this is achieved, and what happens in the process, takes us to the outer regions of the Tsar's kingdom and the inner reaches of his daughters' bodily identity. A tricky subject is treated with the lightest touch and a steady flow of humour.

Pushkin's novel in verse, *Yevgeny Onegin*, cannot be adequately treated here; it is too long and expansive, too stylish and too dependent on its special form—366 stanzas in a specially designed version of the sonnet—to survive encapsulation. Since this is his finest single work, however, we have included a few sample stanzas from the middle of the novel to give a general idea of how the form works.

Fifteen lyric poems stand for the eight hundred plus that Pushkin has left behind. They cover a number of his commonest preoccupations, including poetry itself and the impact of inspiration; love and sex, which played a large part in Pushkin's life; short tales of folk interest; and the natural scene, which is widely described in many of Pushkin's works. The last poem is a Russian version of *Exegi Monumentum*, in which the Roman poet Horace states his confidence that he will be remembered by posterity. Pushkin has nothing to fear from this warning found in a reference book: "Only the likes of a Horace should apply this sentence to their own works."

ANTHONY BRIGGS

14

THE QUEEN OF SPADES

The Queen of Spades has a hidden meaning—bad blood.

Fortune-Telling Companion,
Latest Edition

I

In all kinds of weather
They sat down together
When able,
And soon—for God's sake!—
They were doubling the stake
At the table.
They marked cards with crosses,
And wrote down their losses
In chalk.
Yes, in all kinds of weather
They got down together
To work.

T HERE WAS ONCE a card game at the residence of Horse Guardsman Narumov. A long winter night had slipped by unnoticed, and it was past four o'clock when they sat down to dine. The winners thoroughly enjoyed their dinner; the others sat there at empty places, unable to concentrate on anything. But champagne was served, the conversation struck up again, and everybody was involved.

"How'd you get on, Surin?" asked the host.

"Lost. I always do. To be honest, I'm just not lucky. I don't take any risks, I never raise the stakes, I don't let anything put me off, and I still end up losing!"

"And you've never been tempted? Never done any doubling up?… Your willpower amazes me."

"Well, what about Hermann?" said one of the guests, gesturing towards a young Engineers officer. "Never picked up a card since the day he was born, never doubled a stake, and he sits here till five in the morning just watching us gamble."

"I'm very interested in gambling," said Hermann, "but I'm in no situation to sacrifice what is essential in the hope of winning something superfluous."

"Hermann's from Germany. He calculates the odds. Nothing more to it than that," put in Tomsky. "If there's one person I *don't* understand, it's my grandmother, Countess Anna Fedotovna."

"Why? What d'you mean?" cried the company.

"What I can't work out," Tomsky went on, "is why my grandmother never has a bet."

"What's so funny about that?" said Narumov. "An old woman of eighty who doesn't gamble?"

"So, you've never heard anything about her?"

"No! Honestly, I haven't. Nothing at all!"

"Oh, well, listen to this. You ought to know that, fifty-odd years ago, my grandmother used to go to Paris, where she was considered the latest thing. People flocked after her to get a glimpse of the 'Venus from Moscow'. Richelieu pursued her, and Grandmother swears he nearly shot himself because of her hard heart. At that time the ladies liked to play faro. One day at court she lost to the Duke of Orléans on credit—it was a large sum of money. Back home, as she peeled off her beauty spots and unfastened her crinoline, Grandmother declared her loss to my grandfather and ordered him to pay it off. My late grandfather, I seem to recall, was like a butler to my grandmother. He dreaded her like fire, but when he heard about this terrible loss of hers he lost his temper, brought out the accounts, pointing out that they had spent half a million in half a year, that living near Paris wasn't the same as living on their own estates near Moscow or Saratov, and refused point-blank to pay. Grandmother slapped his face and went off to bed alone as a sign of her displeasure. The next morning she sent for her husband, hoping that marital punishment would have had its effect on him, but she found him intransigent. For the first time in her life she was reduced to persuasion and argument with him; her idea was to bring him to heel by deigning to point out that there are different kinds of debt, and that there is a difference between a prince and a coach-builder. No use! Grandfather was in revolt. Nothing more to be said. Grandmother had no idea what to do.

"She numbered among her acquaintances one quite remarkable man. You will have heard the name of Count Saint-Germain, about whom such wonderful stories are told. You will know that he had claimed to be the Wandering Jew, the discoverer of the elixir of life, and the philosopher's stone, and so on. He was ridiculed as a charlatan, but Casanova in his memoirs refers to him as a spy. Putting that aside, Saint-Germain, for all his air of mystery, had a handsome look about him and a charismatic personality. To this day Grandmother loves him to distraction, and she gets angry when disrespectful things are said about him. Grandmother knew that he had access to big money. Deciding to throw herself on his mercy, she wrote him a note asking him to come round and see her without delay. The old eccentric lost no time in getting there, and found her prostrate with grief. She described her husband's barbarity in the darkest terms, and ended by placing all her hopes on his friendship and generosity.

"Saint-Germain gave it some thought. 'I can oblige you with that sum of money,' he said, 'but I know you will never rest until you have been able to pay me back, and I wouldn't wish to cause you any more trouble. There is another solution: you can win it all back.'

"'But, my dear Count,' Grandmother replied, 'I'm telling you—we have no money at all.'

"'Money is not required,' replied Saint-Germain. 'Please let me finish.'

"At this point he told her a secret that any of us would pay a good deal to learn…"

The young gamblers redoubled their interest. Tomsky lit his pipe, pulled on it, and spoke further.

"That same evening Grandmother turned up at the *Jeu de la Reine* in Versailles. The Duke of Orléans was dealing. Grandmother muttered a word of apology for not bringing the money to pay off her debt, concocting a little story by way of excuse, and she began to bet against him. She chose three cards, and played them one after the other; all three won at the first turn of the cards, doubling up in series, and Grandmother had recouped her entire debt."

"Fluke!" said one of the guests.

"Fairy tale!" cried Hermann.

"Could have been marked cards," was the response from a third guest, eager to join in.

"I think not," observed Tomsky with some gravity.

"What?" said Narumov. "You have a grandmother who can play three winning cards in a row, and in all this time you haven't got hold of her magic formula?"

"Not much chance of that!" replied Tomsky. "She had four sons, one of them being my father. They were all desperate gamblers, and she never told her secret to any one of them, even though it could have done them a lot of good, and me, too, for that matter. But my uncle, Count Ivan Ilyich, told me something which he swore was true. That man Chaplitsky—he's dead now, squandered millions and died in poverty—in his youth once lost about three hundred thousand—to Zorich, if memory serves. He was in despair. Grandmother always came down hard on young people's stupid indiscretions, but for some reason she took pity on Chaplitsky. She told him the three cards, provided that he played them in the right sequence and gave his word never to gamble again. Chaplitsky turned up to face his victorious opponent;

they sat down to play. Chaplitsky staked fifty thousand on the first card—a straight win—and by doubling and redoubling he recouped all his losses, with a bit left over…

"Anyway, it's bedtime. A quarter to six."

Yes, indeed, it was getting light. The young men downed their drinks and went their separate ways.

II

"Il paraît que monsieur est décidément pour les suivantes."
"Que voulez-vous, madame? Elles sont les plus fraîches."*

From a society conversation

Old Countess —— was sitting in her dressing room, facing the mirror. She was surrounded by three maids. One was holding a pot of rouge; another, a box of hairpins; and the third, a tall cap with flame-coloured ribbons. The Countess had not the slightest pretension to a beauty now long-faded, but she had retained all the habits of her young days; she was a slave to the fashions of the Seventies, and she took just as long, and just as much care, over her *toilette* as she had done sixty years before.

---

* "It appears that monsieur has a distinct preference for ladies' maids."

"What do you expect, madam? There's nothing fresher." (French.)

Over by the window, at an embroidery frame, sat a young woman, her ward.

"Hello, *grand'maman!*" said a young man, walking in. "*Bonjour, Mademoiselle Lise. Grand'maman,* I've come to ask a favour."

"What's that, Paul?"

"Would you please allow me to introduce one of my friends, and bring him to see you at the ball on Friday evening?"

"Just bring him to the ball, and then you can introduce him. Were you at ——'s last night?'

"Oh, yes! We had a marvellous time. Still dancing at five o'clock. Yeletskaya looked so attractive."

"Oh, my dear child. Is there anything attractive about her? You should have seen her grandmother, Princess Darya Petrovna... By the way, I imagine she must have aged quite a bit, Princess Darya Petrovna, hasn't she?"

"Aged?" asked Tomsky, his thoughts miles away. "She's been dead these last seven years."

The young lady looked up and sent a signal to the young man. He remembered that they had been hiding the deaths of the old Countess's contemporaries from her, and he bit his lip. But the Countess heard the news with the utmost indifference.

"Dead?" she said, "And I didn't know. We were appointed maids of honour at the same time, and just as we were being presented..."

And, for the benefit of her grandson, the Countess launched forth into her story for the hundredth time.

"Well, Paul," she said eventually. "Now you must help me up. Lizanka, where is my snuffbox?"

And the Countess disappeared behind a screen with her three maids to finish dressing. Tomsky stayed outside with the young lady.

"Who is it you want to introduce?" asked Lizaveta Ivanovna in a low voice.

"Narumov. Do you know him?"

"No. Military or civilian?"

"Military."

"In the Engineers?"

"No, he's in the Horse Guards. Why did you think he was an Engineer?"

The young lady gave a light laugh, and said nothing in reply.

"Paul!" the Countess called out from behind the screen. "Send me another novel, but not one of those modern ones."

"What do you mean, *grand'maman*?"

"I mean a novel in which the hero doesn't strangle his father or his mother, and there aren't any drowned bodies. I cannot abide drowned bodies."

"There aren't any novels like that nowadays. Do you want *Russian* novels?"

"Are there any?… Send me something, sir, just send it."

"Sorry, *grand'maman*, I'm in a bit of a hurry… Excuse

me, Lizaveta Ivanovna! But why did you think Narumov was an Engineer?"

And Tomsky walked out of the dressing room.

Lizaveta Ivanovna, left on her own, abandoned her work and turned to look out of the window. It wasn't long before a young officer came round the corner house on the other side of the street. Her cheeks reddened; she took up her work again, bending over her canvas. At this moment the Countess emerged, fully dressed.

"Lizanka," she said. "Order the carriage. Let's go for a drive."

Liza stood up from her frame, and started collecting her work.

"My dear girl, are you deaf?" cried the Countess. "Order the carriage *now*."

"Yes, madam," said the young lady in a muted reply, and she ran out into the entrance hall.

A servant came in and handed the Countess some books from Prince Paul.

"Jolly good! Send my thanks," said the Countess. "Lizanka, Lizanka, where are you running off to?"

"I'm going to get dressed."

"Plenty of time, my dear. Stay where you are. Open the first volume and read to me…"

The young lady opened the book and read a few lines.

"Louder!" said the Countess. "What's wrong with you, child? Have you lost your voice?… Wait a minute… move that footstool closer… a bit more… That's it!"

Lizaveta Ivanovna read a couple more pages. The Countess gave a yawn.

"Get rid of that book," she said. "It's all nonsense! Send it back to Prince Paul with my thanks... Right, where's my carriage?"

"The carriage is ready," said Lizaveta Ivanovna, looking out into the street.

"Why aren't you dressed for going out?" said the Countess. "I'm always having to wait for you! It's intolerable, young lady!"

Liza sped off to her room. Before two minutes had passed the Countess was ringing as loud as could be. Three maids rushed in through one door, and a footman through the other.

"Can't you hear me calling?" the Countess said to them. "Tell Lizaveta Ivanovna that I'm waiting."

Lizaveta Ivanovna came in wearing a cloak and hat.

"At last, my dear girl!" said the Countess. "All dressed up, I see!... What's this for?... Trying to attract someone?... What's the weather like? Windy, I suppose?"

"Not all, Your Ladyship! It's very still!" answered the footman.

"You always say the first thing that comes into your head!... Open that little window... I told you so—it's windy! And freezing cold! Send the carriage away. Lizanka, we're not going out. There was no need to get all dolled up."

"And this is my life," thought Lizaveta Ivanovna.

And indeed, Lizaveta Ivanovna was a truly miserable creature. How salt is the taste of another's bread, said Dante, and how hard it is going up and down another's stairs—and who has a better understanding of dependence than the poor ward of a grande dame? Countess ——was not, of course, a wicked person, but she was a capricious woman, spoilt by life in high society, tight-fisted and drowning in frigid egoism, like all old people whose affections have drained away with advancing age, leaving them alienated from the present day. She was a full participant in all high-society frivolities, taking herself off to every ball, where she sat things out in a corner, rouged up and dressed in the fashions of yesteryear, like a hideous but indispensable ballroom ornament. New arrivals came forward to grovel before her, acting out a kind of ancient, ritual performance, after which she was totally ignored. She was at home to the whole city, observing etiquette down to the last detail, without actually recognizing anyone. Her innumerable domestic staff, grown fat and grey-haired in the entrance hall and servants' quarters, did what she wanted while competitively fleecing the moribund old woman. Lizaveta Ivanovna was the household martyr. She poured the tea, and was told off for wasting sugar; she read novels aloud, and the authors' mistakes were all her fault; when she went out with the Countess, she was held responsible for the weather and the state of the pavements. She was supposed to receive an allowance, but it was never paid in full; even so, she was expected to be dressed like everybody else, which meant like very few others. Out in society she played the most pathetic role imaginable. Everybody knew who she was, but she was universally ignored; at balls she danced only when a vis-à-vis was needed, and the ladies were all over her only when they needed to withdraw to adjust their attire. Proud and sensitively aware of her position, she looked round, longing for someone to come and rescue her, but the young men, full of calculation for all their giddiness and vanity, simply ignored her, even though Lizaveta Ivanovna was a hundred times more attractive than the brazen, frigid young girls on whom they danced attendance. How often did she sneak away from the tedious luxury of the ballroom to go and weep in her poor little room with its wallpapered screen, chest of drawers, little mirror and painted bedstead, where a tallow candle guttered dimly on its brass stand.

One day—this occurred two days after the evening described at the beginning of this story, and a week before the scene on which we have just ended—one day Lizaveta Ivanovna, seated at her embroidery frame by the window, happened to glance down into the street, where she saw a young Engineers officer standing there, looking up attentively at her window. She lowered her gaze, and got back to work; five minutes later she looked down again, and the officer was still there in the same place. Unaccustomed to flirtation with passing officers, she stopped looking down at the street, and carried on sewing for two hours without looking up. The call came for dinner. She got to her feet and was beginning to put away her embroidery when she happened to glance down at the street and saw the officer once again. This seemed rather strange. When dinner was over she went to the window with a feeling of some trepidation, but the officer had gone—and she put him out of her mind…

A couple of days later, as she walked out with the Countess to get into the carriage, she saw him again. He was standing right by the entry, with his face buried in a beaver collar, and black eyes gleaming under his hat. Lizaveta Ivanovna was shocked without knowing why, and she got into the carriage, shivering for no good reason. Once back home, she rushed across to the window—and the officer was standing in the same place, staring up at her. She backed away, tormented by curiosity and excitement—a completely new feeling.

From then on, not a day passed without the young officer appearing at a fixed time in front of the windows. A relationship built up spontaneously between the two of them. As she sat there at her work she could sense him approaching; she would look up from her work and glance down at him—a little longer every day. The young man seemed to be grateful to her; with the sharp eyes of youth she could make out a rapid flush that crossed his pale cheeks every time their eyes met. Within a week she had smiled at him…

When Tomsky had asked permission to introduce a friend to the Countess, the young girl's heart had leapt.

But once she knew that Narumov was not in the Engineers, but in the Horse Guards, she was sorry to think that her indiscreet question had given away her secret to the volatile Tomsky.

Hermann was the son of a Russified German, who had left him a little capital. Deeply convinced of the need to ensure his independence, Hermann didn't even touch the interest on this money; he lived on his salary alone, allowing himself nothing in the way of luxury. He was, however, both reserved and ambitious, and his friends had little opportunity to make fun of his undue parsimony. He was a man of strong passions and vivid imagination, but his resolute nature saved him from the usual vagaries of youth. For instance, despite being a gambler at heart he never picked up a card, because he had calculated that, in his own words, his situation did not allow him "to sacrifice what is essential in the hope of winning something superfluous". This did not stop him spending night after night at the card tables, watching the twists and turns of the game with feverish excitement.

The story of the three cards had really captured his imagination, and all night long he couldn't get it out of his mind. "What if…" he kept thinking the next evening as he roamed the streets of Petersburg, "What if the old Countess were to give me her secret—tell me the three winning cards? Why not give it a go?… Get myself introduced, play up to her, maybe even become her lover? But it all takes time, and she's eighty-seven years old, she could die within a week, or a couple of days!... Yes, and what about that story?... Is it believable?... No, my three winning cards are caution, moderation and hard work; they are what will bring me three times, seven times, my capital, and give me peace of mind and independence!" While he was thinking along these lines he suddenly found himself on one of the main streets of Petersburg, right in front of a house of ancient architecture. The street was crammed with traffic as one carriage after another rolled up at the illuminated front steps. From the carriages, minute by minute, feet came stepping down: the shapely foot of a young girl, a jingling jackboot, a striped stocking or a diplomatic slipper. Hermann came to a halt.

"Whose house is this?" he asked the watchman on the corner.

"Belongs to Countess ———," the watchman replied.

Hermann shivered. The amazing story came back to his imagination. He began walking up and down outside the house, thinking about its owner and her miraculous ability. When he got back to his modest little room he could not get to sleep for a long time, and when he did drop off he kept dreaming about cards, a green table, piles of notes and heaps of gold coins. He bet on card after card, bent the corners with a firm hand, doubling his stake, and he went on winning and winning, raking in the gold and stuffing notes into his pockets. It was late when he woke up, sighing for the loss of that fantastic wealth, and when he went out again to roam the city he soon found himself outside the Countess's house once again. An unknown power seemed to be drawing him back there all the time. He stopped and began to look up at the windows. At one of them he could see the dark hair of a small head bending down, probably over a book or some kind of work. The small head looked up. Hermann saw a fresh-looking face with black eyes. That moment sealed his fate.

III

Vous m'écrivez, mon ange, des letters de quatre pages plus vite que je ne puis les lire.[*]

From a correspondence

Lizaveta Ivanovna had scarcely managed to take off her cloak and hat when the Countess sent for her and ordered the carriage to be brought round again. They went to get in. At the very moment when two footmen half-lifted the Countess and bundled her in through the carriage door, Lizaveta Ivanovna caught sight of her Engineers officer

---

[*] You write four-page letters, my angel, faster than I can read them. (French.)

alongside the wheel. He seized her by the hand, and she was frightened almost out of her wits; the young man disappeared leaving a letter in her hand. She hid it in her glove, and throughout the whole journey she heard and saw nothing at all. It was the Countess's habit to ask questions all the time when they were out in the carriage. Who was that we just met? What's the name of that bridge? What does it say on that sign? On this occasion Lizaveta Ivanovna's answers were irrelevant and absurd, which infuriated the Countess.

"What's the matter with you, young lady? Have you taken leave of your senses? You're either not listening to me, or you don't understand. Good heavens, girl, I don't speak with a lisp, and I'm not yet out of my mind!"

Lizaveta Ivanovna wasn't listening. When they got home she rushed back to her room, and took the letter out from the glove—it was unsealed. Lizaveta Ivanovna read it. The letter contained a declaration of love; it was written with tenderness and respect, and copied word for word from a German novel. But Lizaveta Ivanovna knew no German, and she was pleased with it.

Still, the letter she had received was a great worry. This was the first time she had entered into a secret and intimate relationship with a young man. His direct approach horrified her. She blamed herself for her own rash behaviour, and didn't know what to do. Should she stop sitting by the window and cool the young officer's desire for further pursuit by ignoring him? Should she send the letter back? Should she send a cold response in no uncertain terms? She had no one to consult; she had no confidante, no older adviser. Lizaveta Ivanovna decided to reply.

She sat down at the writing table, took hold of pen and paper—and thought things over. She began writing her letter more than once, but tore it up each time: her words seemed either too snooty or too brutal. At last, she managed to write a few lines that she could be pleased with. "I am sure," she wrote, "that your intentions are honourable and that you did not intend to offend me by a thoughtless action. But our acquaintance ought not to begin in this manner. I am returning your letter, and I hope that in future I shall have no cause to complain about disrespect that is unmerited."

The next morning, when she caught sight of Hermann walking by, Lizaveta Ivanovna got up from her embroidery, went down into the hall, opened the little ventilation window and threw the letter out into the street, counting on the young officer's readiness. Hermann ran across, picked it up and disappeared into a patisserie. He broke the seal and discovered his own letter and Lizaveta Ivanovna's reply. This was what he had expected and he walked back home, absorbed in his plot.

Three days later a note was delivered to Lizaveta Ivanovna by a bright-eyed slip of a girl from the milliner's shop. Lizaveta Ivanovna opened it with some trepidation, expecting a bill, but suddenly she recognized Hermann's handwriting.

"You've got it wrong, my dear," she said, "This note isn't for me."

"Oh, yes, it is!" replied the sharp young girl without disguising a sly smile. "Be so good as to read it."

Lizaveta Ivanovna read the note hurriedly. Hermann was asking for a rendezvous.

"It's not possible," said Lizaveta Ivanovna, shocked by the audacity of the demand and the method employed. "This doesn't seem to be meant for me."

And she tore the letter up into small pieces.

"If it's not for you, why have you torn it up?" asked the young miss. "I could have taken it back to the sender."

"My dear girl, *please*!" said Lizaveta Ivanovna, blushing at this remark. "Don't bring me any more notes. And tell the man who sent you he should be ashamed of himself…"

But Hermann was not put off. Every day Lizaveta Ivanovna received a letter from him by one means or another. They were not now translated from German. Hermann wrote them himself, passionately inspired, and he wrote in his own way; they were an expression of his determination, his desire and the confusion of his unbridled imagination. It no longer occurred to Lizaveta Ivanovna to return them; she thoroughly enjoyed them and began to reply. Her notes to him became longer and sweeter by the hour. At last she dropped the following letter to him out through the window:

Tonight there is a ball at the —— Embassy. The Countess will be there. We shall stay until two o'clock. This is your chance to see me alone. As soon as the Countess leaves, her servants are sure to go off duty. The porter will still be there at the lodge, but he usually goes off into his room. Make your way in at half past eleven. Go straight up the staircase. If you meet anyone in the hall just ask whether the Countess is at home. They will say "No", and that's it—you will have to go home. But you probably won't meet anybody. The maids stay in their own room. Turn left out of the hall and go straight on towards the Countess's bedroom. In the bedroom you will find two little doors behind a screen. On the right there is a study where the Countess never goes; on the left there is a passage and a little spiral staircase leading to my room.

Hermann trembled like a tiger as he waited for the appointed time. He was outside the Countess's house by ten o'clock in the evening. The weather was foul, with a howling wind and snow falling in wet flakes. The lamps shone dimly; the streets were deserted. Now and again a cab went by, drawn by a skinny nag, with the driver on the lookout for a late-night fare. Hermann stood there without an overcoat, but insensitive to wind or snow. At last the Countess's carriage was brought round. Hermann watched the footmen come out, half-carrying the bent old woman wrapped up warm in her sable coat, and he caught a glimpse of her young ward emerging behind her, her hair done up with fresh flowers and wearing a thin wrap. The carriage doors closed with a clunk. The vehicle trundled off over the wet snow. The porter closed the front door. The lights went out. Hermann paced up and down outside the deserted house. He went to a street lamp and looked at his watch—it said twenty minutes past eleven. He stood there under the lamp with his eyes fixed on the minute hand, waiting for the remaining time to pass. At exactly half past eleven Hermann walked up the Countess's steps, through the porch and into the brightly lit vestibule. There was no porter. Hermann nipped up the staircase, opened a door into the hall, and saw a servant asleep under a lamp in a tatty old armchair. Hermann walked past him with a light, determined stride. The ballroom and drawing room were in darkness. A lamp in the hall gave them some dim light. Hermann entered the bedroom. A golden lamp burned before a stand covered with ancient icons. Faded brocade armchairs and sofas with fluffy cushions of worn gilt, stood in sad symmetry before walls decorated with Chinese wallpaper. On one wall there were two portraits painted in Paris by Mme Lebrun. One of them showed a man of about forty, red in the face and rather stout, wearing a bright-green uniform and a star; the other depicted a young beauty with an aquiline nose, her powdered hair combed back and set off with a rose. All the corners were noticeably adorned with porcelain shepherdesses, table clocks done by the famous Leroy, little boxes, bandalores, fans and ladies' toys invented at the end of the last century along with the

Montgolfiers' balloon and Mesmer's animal magnetism. Hermann went round the screen. Behind it there was a small iron bedstead; on the right was a door leading to the study, on the left another one into the passage. Hermann opened this one, and saw a narrow spiral staircase, leading up to the poor young ward's room… But… he came back out, and walked into the dark study.

Time was passing slowly. It was very quiet. In the drawing room a clock struck twelve; in all the rooms, one after another, the clocks chimed the midnight hour, and then—silence fell again. Hermann stood still, leaning against the cold stove. He was calm. His heart beat steadily like that of man determined to carry out a dangerous but necessary assignment. The clocks chimed one, and two, and then he heard the rumble of a distant carriage. He was seized with a feeling of agitation. The carriage drew up and stopped. He heard them lower the steps. Indoors, things came to life. Servants ran in, voices were heard and the house was busy. Three old lady's maids came into the bedroom, and then the Countess, more dead than alive, followed them in and flopped down into a large Voltaire armchair. Hermann peered through a crack. Lizaveta Ivanovna walked right past him. Hermann heard her rapid footsteps going up her staircase. His heart shrank with something akin to remorse, but it soon died away. He was hardened to his purpose.

The Countess began to undress in front of the mirror. Her bonnet with its flowers was unpinned. Her powdered wig was removed from her grey, close-cropped head. Pins showered down around her. The yellow dress, embroidered with silver, fell at her swollen feet. Hermann was witness to the disgusting secrets of her *toilette*; then, at last, the Countess was left in her bed-jacket and nightcap. In this attire, more suited to her age, she looked less ugly and repellent.

Like all old people, the Countess suffered from insomnia. Now she was undressed, she sat down by the window in the Voltaire armchair and dismissed the maids. The candles were taken away, and once again the room was lit only by the little lamp. The Countess sat there, all yellow, her flabby lips champing, rocking right and left. Her dull eyes marked the absence of all thought. Looking at her, one might have thought that the rocking of the old woman came not from her own will, but from the action of some secret galvanic mechanism.

Suddenly an inexplicable change came over her dead face. The lips stopped champing, the eyes lit up. An unknown man stood there before the Countess.

"Don't be afraid! For heaven's sake, you mustn't be afraid!" he said in a low, clear voice. "I'm not going to hurt you. I've come to ask a favour."

The old woman looked at him in silence; it was as if she couldn't hear him. Hermann, assuming she must be deaf, bent down close to the ear itself and repeated what he had said. The Countess said nothing, as before.

"You have it in your power," Hermann went on, "to complete my happiness, and it won't cost you anything. I know that you can guess three cards to be played in sequence…"

Hermann stopped. The Countess seemed to have understood what was being asked of her. She seemed to be searching for words to reply.

"That was a joke," she said at last. "I swear it was a joke!"

"It's not a joking matter." Hermann rounded on her angrily. "Remember Chaplitsky. You helped him recoup."

The Countess was visibly disturbed. Her features reflected a deep stirring of her spirit… But she soon relapsed into her earlier insensitivity.

"Can you please tell me?" Hermann went on. "Tell me the three winning cards!"

The Countess said nothing. Hermann went on again.

"For whom are you keeping this secret? Your grand-children? They're already rich. And they don't know the value of money. Your three cards won't help anyone who wastes money. A man who cannot look after his own inheritance is going to die in poverty anyway, whatever demonic powers he uses. I don't waste money. Your three cards will not go amiss with me. Listen to me!…"

He stopped, and waited, quivering, for her to respond. The Countess said nothing. Hermann went down on his knees.

"If ever your heart," he said, "has known the feeling of love, if you can remember its delights, if even once you have smiled at the cry of a new baby boy, if any human warmth has throbbed within you, then I appeal to your feelings as a wife, a lover, a mother, by all that is sacred in life, not to ignore my plea! Tell me your secret! What does it mean to you now?... Maybe it is linked somehow to a terrible sin, the loss of eternal bliss, a pact with the devil... Think about it. You are old; you haven't long to live. I am ready to take your sins onto my soul. Just tell me your secret. Think about it. You hold a man's happiness in your hands. It goes beyond me. My children, grandchildren, great-grandchildren will bless and respect your memory, holding it sacred..."

Not a word of reply came from the Countess.

Hermann got to his feet.

"You old witch!" he said through gritted teeth. "All right... I'll force a reply out of you!..."

With these words he took a pistol out of his pocket. When she saw the pistol the Countess showed strong emotion for the second time. She looked up and raised her hand as if to ward off the shot... then she fell down on her back... and lay there without moving.

"Stop playing about," said Hermann, taking her hand. "I'm asking you for the last time. Will you tell me your three cards? Yes or no?"

No answer came from the Countess. Hermann saw that she was dead.

IV

7 mai 18—
*Homme sans mœurs et sans religion!**

Lizaveta Ivanovna sat in her room, still in her ball gown, deep in thought. As soon as she returned home she lost no time in dismissing her sleepy-eyed servant-girl, who had grudgingly offered her services, by saying that she would get undressed on her own, and she went to her room in some trepidation, hoping to find Hermann there and wanting not to. It took the merest glance for her to determine his absence, and she thanked her lucky stars for whatever obstacle had prevented their meeting. She sat down without taking off her things, and began to recall all the developments which had taken her so far in such a short time. It was less than three weeks since she had first seen the young man from her window—and here she was already corresponding with him, and he had talked her into a late-night meeting with her! She knew his name simply because a number of his letters were signed with it. She had never spoken to him, never heard his voice, never heard anything about him… until this very evening.

---

* 7th May 18—. A man with no morals or religion! (French.)

What a strange turn of events! That same evening, at the ball, Tomsky, stung by young Princess Pauline, who for once in her life had been flirting with someone other than him, wanted to get his own back with a display of indifference. He had summoned Lizaveta Ivanovna and danced the continuous mazurka with her. He had spent the whole time ribbing her about her predilection for Engineers officers, intimating that he knew a good deal more than she could possibly imagine, and some of his barbs were so neatly directed that several times Lizaveta Ivanovna thought that he was privy to her secret.

"Who told you all these things that you know?" she asked with a laugh.

"The friend of a person well known to you," answered Tomsky. "A very remarkable man!"

"Well, who is this remarkable man?"

"His name is Hermann."

Lizaveta Ivanovna gave not a word of reply, but her hands and feet had turned to ice.

"This Hermann," Tomsky went on, "is a truly Romantic figure. He has the profile of Napoleon and the soul of Mephistopheles. It's my belief that he has at least three crimes on his conscience. You do seem to have gone pale!…"

"I have a headache… What has he been saying to you, this Hermann… or whatever his name is?…"

"Hermann is greatly displeased with his friend. He says that *he* would have acted quite differently… I'd go so far

43

as to say that Hermann has designs on you. Anyway, he listens to the lovelorn exclamations from his friend with anything but indifference."

"But where has he seen me?"

"At church, perhaps. Or outside, taking the air!… Heaven knows where! Perhaps in your room while you were asleep. He's capable of anything…"

The conversation, which had become painfully intriguing for Lizaveta Ivanovna, was interrupted by three ladies who came up to them to ask "*oubli ou regret?*".

The lady chosen by Tomsky was none other than Princess Pauline. She managed a reconciliation with him in the time taken for one more turn round the floor and one more spin in front of her chair, and by the time Tomsky got back to his place he no longer had Hermann or Lizaveta Ivanovna in mind. She desperately wanted to take up the interrupted conversation, but the mazurka came to an end, and it wasn't long before the Countess left to go home.

Tomsky's words had been nothing more than mazurka chit-chat, but they had struck home with the fanciful young lady. The portrait sketched out by Tomsky had coincided with the picture which she herself had put together, and, thanks to the effect of modern novels, this type of person, by now a vulgar commonplace, was sure to capture her imagination and filled her with alarm. She sat there, with her bare arms crossed and her head, still decked with flowers, bowed over her naked bosom… Then suddenly the door opened, and in came Hermann. She shuddered.

"Where have you been?" she asked in a frightened whisper.

"In the bedroom with the old Countess," Hermann replied. "I've just been there. The Countess is dead."

"Good heavens! What are you saying?"

"And it seems," went on Hermann, "that I was the cause of her death."

Lizaveta Ivanovna glanced at him, and Tomsky's words echoed in her mind: *this man has at least three crimes on his conscience*! Hermann sat down on the window sill and told her the whole story.

Lizaveta Ivanovna listened with horror. So, those passionate letters, the ardent demands, this bold and determined pursuit of her—had nothing to do with love. Money! That's what his soul was aching for! It was not for her to satisfy his desire and make him happy! Poor ward that she was, she was no more than the blind accessory of a criminal, the murderer of her old benefactress!… She wept bitter tears of belated, agonizing remorse. Hermann looked at her in silence. His heart was breaking too, but his hardened spirit was moved neither by a young girl's tears nor by her surprising beauty in all the grief. It wasn't that the old woman's death had left him conscience-stricken. He was horrified by only one thing: the irretrievable loss of the secret he had been counting on to get rich.

"You're a monster!" said Lizaveta Ivanovna at last.

"I didn't mean to kill her," replied Hermann. "The pistol wasn't loaded."

Neither of them spoke.

Morning was coming on. Lizaveta Ivanovna put out the guttering candle. Thin daylight brightened her room. She wiped her tear-stained eyes and looked up at Hermann. He was sitting on the window sill with his arms folded and a grim scowl on his face. In this position he did look remarkably like a picture of Napoleon. The similarity certainly struck Lizaveta Ivanovna.

"How are you going to get out of the building?" said Lizaveta Ivanovna at last. "I meant to take you out down the secret staircase, but that means going past the bedroom, and I'm too scared."

"Tell me how to find the secret staircase, and I'll go out that way."

Lizaveta Ivanovna got up, took a key out of a drawer, and gave it to Hermann along with detailed instructions. Hermann squeezed her cold, unresponsive hand, kissed the top of her bowed head, and left. He went down the spiral staircase, and back into the Countess's bedroom. The dead woman sat there as stiff as stone, her face registering a sense of deep peace. Hermann stopped in front of her, and looked at her for a long time as if to confirm the terrible truth. At last he went into the study, felt his way to a door behind the tapestry, and set off down a dark staircase, full of strange emotions. "Creeping up these very stairs," he thought, "maybe sixty years ago, some happy youth, long since mouldering in his grave, would have gone through into that same bedroom at a

46

time like this, dressed in an embroidered tunic, with his hair done *à l'oiseau royal*, clutching a three-cornered hat to his breast; and the heart of his ancient lover has stopped beating only today…'

At the bottom of the stairs Hermann came to another door, which opened with the same key, and soon found himself in a passageway leading out onto the street.

V

That same night the late Baroness von V——
appeared to me. She was all in white, and she said
to me, "Hello, Mr Councillor."

Swedenborg

Three days after the fateful night, at ten in the evening, Hermann set off for the Convent of M——, where last respects would be paid to the deceased Countess. While feeling no remorse, he couldn't entirely silence the voice of conscience, which kept saying to him, "You murdered the old woman." A man of little true faith, he was full of superstition. He believed that the dead Countess might still have a baleful influence on his life, and he had decided to turn up at her funeral to ask and obtain her forgiveness.

The church was full. Hermann had difficulty in forcing his way through the crowd. The coffin stood on an opulent catafalque, beneath a canopy of velvet. The dead woman lay inside it with her arms crossed over her breast, dressed in her lace nightcap and a white satin robe. Members of the household stood round about: servants in their long black coats with armorial ribbons at the shoulder and candles in their hands. The relatives were in deep mourning—children, grandchildren and great-grandchildren. No one was weeping; tears would have been *une affectation*. The Countess had been so old that her death had not come as a shock to anyone, and for some time now her relatives had been looking on her as a relic of a bygone age. A young bishop gave the funeral oration. In simple, moving phrases he recounted the peaceful passing of a pious woman, whose long years had been a steady, heart-warming preparation for a Christian end. "The angel of death," said the speaker, "found her vigilant in pious thoughts, in expectation of the midnight bridegroom." The service proceeded to its end with melancholic decorum. Relatives were the first to come forward and take their leave of the corpse. After them came the many guests who had driven there to pay their respects to a woman who had for so long been a participant in their frivolous round of amusements. They were followed by all the domestics. Right at the end came an old woman servant of the same age as the Countess. Two young girls brought her along, propping her up. Although not strong enough to bow right down to the ground, she was the only person to shed any tears when she kissed her old mistress's cold hand. Hermann decided to go up to the coffin after her. He bowed to the ground, and for some minutes he lay there on the cold floor, which was strewn with fir twigs. At last he got to his feet, as pale as the dead woman herself, climbed the steps of the catafalque, and bent forward… At that moment it seemed to him that the deceased woman was looking at him mockingly and winking with one eye. Hermann stepped away with a start, lost his footing and fell down heavily onto his back. He was helped to his feet. At the same time, Lizaveta Ivanovna was carried out into the porch in a dead faint. For a few minutes this incident disturbed the solemnity of the sad occasion. A stifled murmur ran through the congregation, and a gaunt chamberlain, closely related to the deceased, whispered into the ear of a young Englishman at his side, letting him know that the young officer was the Countess's illegitimate son, to which the Englishman replied with a cold, "Oh?"

All that day Hermann was deeply troubled. He took his dinner in a solitary tavern, and, contrary to his custom, drank a lot, hoping to stifle his inner agitation. But the wine only excited his fevered imagination all the more. He went back home, flung himself onto his bed without taking any clothes off, and fell into a deep sleep.

It was night-time when he woke up, and the moonlight was shining into the room. He glanced at his watch: a quarter to three. Sleep had left him. He sat on the bed, thinking about the old Countess's funeral.

Just then someone glanced in at him through the window, and immediately went away again. Hermann ignored this. A minute later he heard the outer door opening. Hermann assumed that his orderly, drunk as usual, was coming back home from a night out. But then he heard unfamiliar footsteps, someone shuffling up in soft shoes. The door opened; in came a woman in a white dress. Hermann mistook her for his old nurse, and he wondered what could have brought her here at this late hour. But the woman in white slipped inside and stood before him. Hermann recognized the Countess!

"I have come to you against my will," she said in a firm voice, "but I am directed to grant your request. A three, a seven and an ace will win for you, played in sequence, provided that you do not bet on more than one of them in twenty-four hours and never in your life do you play again. I forgive you my death, on condition that you get married to my ward, Lizaveta Ivanovna…"

This said, she turned quietly away, walked to the door and disappeared, shuffling out in her soft shoes. Hermann heard the outer door closing, and saw someone glancing in at him again through the window.

It took some time for Hermann to pull himself together. He went into the other room. His orderly was asleep on the floor; Hermann woke him up with some difficulty. The orderly was drunk, as usual; no sense could be got out of him. The outer door was shut. Hermann went back into his room, lit a candle and wrote down his vision.

"Attendez!"
"How dare you say Attendez *to me?"*
"Your Excellency, what I said was, Attendez, sir.*"*

Two fixed ideas cannot coexist in the moral world just as two bodies in the physical world cannot occupy the same space. "Three, seven, ace" soon drove the image of the dead Countess out of Hermann's mind. "Three, seven, ace" refused to leave his head; they stayed, trembling on his lips.

If he saw a young girl, he would say, "Isn't she lovely? A real three of hearts." If someone asked him the time he would answer, "Five to the seven." Any corpulent man reminded him of the ace. "Three, seven, ace" pursued him even in his sleep, taking on all possible forms. Three blossomed before him in the image of a huge, showy flower; seven took on the form of a Gothic portal; the ace was a huge spider. His thoughts all came together into a single idea—how to take advantage of the secret that had cost him so much. He began to think of retiring from the army and travelling the world. He wanted to go to the public gambling halls of Paris, and wrest riches from the magical grasp of Fortune. Chance saved him the trouble.

A society of wealthy gamblers had been set up in Moscow under the chairmanship of the celebrated Chekalinsky, a man who had spent his whole life with cards, earning himself millions by accepting IOUs when he won but paying in cash when he lost. Long experience had established him as trustworthy among his friends, while an open house, a first-rate chef, a friendly nature and a cheerful personality had secured the public's respect. He had now come to Petersburg. Young people flocked to see him, abandoning the ballroom for the card table, and preferring the temptations of faro to the pleasures of courtship. Narumov brought Hermann to his house.

They walked through a suite of splendid rooms, which were full of attentive servants. All the rooms were teeming with people. One or two generals and privy councillors were playing whist; young people lounged about on damask sofas, eating ices and smoking pipes. In the drawing room the host was sitting at a long table, keeping bank against a couple of dozen punters crowding round. He was a man of sixty or so, very distinguished-looking, with a head of silvery hair and a round, fresh face, exuding bonhomie; his eyes sparkled and a bright smile never left him. Narumov introduced Hermann. Chekalinsky extended a friendly hand, invited him to feel at home with them, and carried on dealing.

The game was a long one. There were more than thirty cards out on the table. Chekalinsky paused after each deal, giving time for the players to sort themselves out, and he would make a note of any losses, generously listening to their requests, and even more generously straightening the odd corner of a card that may have been bent over inadvertently. Eventually the game came to an end. Chekalinsky shuffled the cards and prepared to start again.

"May I place a bet?" said Hermann, reaching past a fat gentleman who was in the game.

Chekalinsky smiled, saying nothing, but he gave a little bow as a polite sign of assent. Narumov smiled too, congratulating Hermann on the end of his long abstinence, and wishing him beginner's luck.

"Here we go!" said Hermann, chalking a huge sum of money on the back of his card.

"How much is that, sir?" asked the banker with a frown. "I'm sorry. I can't quite make it out."

"Forty-seven thousand," Hermann replied.

At these words every head turned in a flash, and all eyes were on Hermann. "He's off his head!" thought Narumov.

"You will allow me to point out," said Chekalinsky with his customary smile, "that this a rather high stake. No one here has ever staked more than two hundred and seventy-five on a single card."

"Well?" Hermann protested. "Do you accept my bet, or not?"

Chekalinsky gave another bow by way of polite assent.

"I just wanted to inform you," he said, "that, honoured as I am by the confidence of my friends, I can play on only for cash. As far as I am concerned personally, I am convinced that your word can be relied on, but in compliance with our rules and systems of accounting, I must ask you to place your money on the card."

Hermann took a banknote from his pocket and handed it to Chekalinsky, who glanced at it and then placed it on Hermann's card.

He began to deal. On the right there was a nine; on the left, a three.

"I win!" said Hermann, turning up his card.

A murmur ran through the gamblers. Chekalinsky gave a frown, though the smile was immediately back on his face.

"Do you wish to settle up?" he asked Hermann.

"If you don't mind."

Chekalinsky took a wad of banknotes from his pocket, and paid out without demur.

Hermann took his money and left the table. Narumov couldn't believe his eyes. Hermann drank a glass of lemonade, and went home.

The following evening he was back at Chekalinsky's. The host was dealing. Hermann came up to the table; the other punters made way for him. Chekalinsky gave him a welcoming bow.

Hermann waited for the next deal, placed his card, and put on it the forty-seven thousand along with yesterday's winnings.

Chekalinsky began to deal. A knave came up on the right; a seven on the left.

Hermann turned up a seven.

Everyone gasped. Chekalinsky was visibly disconcerted. He counted out ninety-four thousand, and gave the money to Hermann. Hermann received it with icy indifference, and left immediately.

The following evening Hermann appeared again at the table. Everyone was waiting for him. The generals and privy councillors abandoned their game of whist in order to watch such an extraordinary form of gambling. The young officers leapt up from their sofas; all the servants also came together in the drawing room. They all crowded in on Hermann. The other gamblers had stopped making bets as they waited eagerly to see how he would fare. Hermann stood at the table, preparing to gamble alone against a pale but still smiling Chekalinsky. Each of them broke open a new pack of cards. Chekalinsky shuffled. Hermann selected his card and placed it on the table, covering it with a stack of banknotes. It was just like a duel. Deep silence prevailed around them.

Chekalinsky began to deal, with shaking hands. On the right was a queen; on the left, an ace.

"My ace wins!" said Hermann, turning his card.

"Your *queen* loses," said Chekalinsky in a kindly voice.

Hermann shuddered; indeed, instead of an ace he held the queen of spades. He couldn't believe his eyes, nor understand how he could have made such a slip.

At that moment he seemed to see the queen of spades winking and smiling at him. He was struck by an extraordinary likeness...

"The old woman!" he cried out in horror.

Chekalinsky raked in the losing banknotes. Hermann stood there making no movement. When he did leave the table a roar of voices erupted.

"Splendid game!" said the gamblers.

Chekalinsky shuffled the cards again. The gambling took its normal course.

Conclusion

Hermann has gone mad. He is now in the Obukhov Hospital (room 17). Refusing to respond to any questions, he keeps up a rapid gabbling: "Three, seven, ace! Three, seven, queen!…"

Lizaveta Ivanovna has married a very nice young man, who works in the Civil Service, and is not without means. He is the son of the Countess's former steward.

Lizaveta Ivanovna is raising a poor young relative as her ward.

Tomsky has been promoted to captain, and he is due to marry Princess Pauline.

THE STATIONMASTER

Government clerk of registration,
Dictator of the postal station

Prince Vyazemsky

W HO HAS NOT CURSED the masters of postal sta-
tions? Who has not had strong words with them?
Who, in a moment of anger, has not demanded from
them the fatal book in which to write down a useless
complaint about harsh treatment at their hands, about
their surliness and unfairness? Who does not consider
them to be monsters in human form, on the level of
legal clerks in old Russia or at least highwaymen in the
forests of Murom? However, in the interests of fairness,
let's put ourselves in their situation; then perhaps we
shall pass judgement on them much more indulgently.
What is a stationmaster? A true martyr of the fourteenth
grade, protected by that rank only from physical assault,
and then not all the time. (Consult your own conscience,
dear readers.) What are the duties of this "dictator",
as he is jokingly called by Prince Vyazemsky? Do they
not amount to actual penal servitude? No peace, day or

night. All the irritations piling up during a boring journey are taken out by the traveller on the stationmaster. Foul weather, terrible roads, difficult drivers, horses that won't pull—it's all his fault. As he enters the stationmaster's miserable abode, the traveller looks on him as an enemy. He's all right as long as he can get rid of his unwanted guest quickly, but if there happen to be no horses... God in heaven, the swearing, the threats that rain down on his head! He has to run round the village through rain and mud, and disappear onto the porch in a storm or the freezing cold to get a moment's respite from the furious traveller's bawling and bashing. Along comes a general—the trembling stationmaster gives him the last two troikas, including the one needed for the mail. The general drives off without a word of thanks. Five minutes later—ding! ding! ding!—and here is an official courier throwing his warrant down on the table!... If you go into all of this at all deeply, your heart will be filled, not with indignation, but with genuine sympathy. And there is more: in the last twenty years, I have travelled across Russia in every direction. Almost all the postal routes are familiar to me; I have got to know several generations of drivers. There aren't many stationmasters whom I don't know by sight; there aren't many with whom I haven't had dealings. In the not too distant future I am hoping to publish an absorbing collection of observations made while travelling. For the moment suffice it to say that the stationmaster class has been grossly misrepresented to the general opinion. These much-maligned masters are, in fact, men of peace; it is in their nature to be accommodating, gregarious, modest in their desire for reward and less mercenary than most. From conversation with them (wrongly neglected by travelling gentlemen) there is much that is curious and instructive to be gleaned. To be honest, as far as I'm concerned, conversation with them is preferable to having discourse with your average sixth-grade official travelling on government business.

You may well have guessed that I have friends within the estimable class of stationmasters. Indeed, there is one among them whose memory is particularly dear. We were once brought together by circumstances, and it is this man that I should like to talk about with my indulgent readers.

It was in May 1816 that I happened to be travelling through the province of ——, along a postal route that has been discontinued. Being of modest rank, I was travelling post and could afford no more than two horses. This meant that the stationmasters didn't put themselves out for me, and I often had to do battle with them to get what I considered to be mine by right. Young and excitable as I was, I didn't mince my words when complaining to a stationmaster about his abject behaviour and spinelessness as the latter was transferring a troika prepared for me to the carriage of a high-ranking government official. It took me just as long to get used to being missed out at the governor's table by a lout of a servant suddenly selective in his favours. Nowadays I take both of these things in my stride. When all's said and done, what would become of us if, instead of the accepted rule, *rank before all*, a new one was introduced—say, *intelligence before all?* Think of the arguments that would arise! And how would servants know whom to serve first? But, back to my story.

It was a hot day. Just over a mile from the station at —— it started to drizzle, and within a minute I was soaked to the skin. When I got to the station my first concern was to change into dry clothes; my second was to order some tea. "Hey, Dunya!" the stationmaster called out. "Put the samovar on, and slip out for some cream, would you?" At these words a young girl, about fourteen years old, ran out from behind the partition and onto the porch. I was struck by her beauty. "Is that your daughter?" I asked the stationmaster. "Yes, sir," he replied with an air of contentment mixed with pride. "And she's such a bright girl, so quick on her feet. Just like her mother, God rest her soul." Then he began copying out the details of my warrant, while I took a close look at the paintings that decorated his humble, but tidy abode. They told the Story of the Prodigal Son. In the first one, a venerable old man in nightcap and dressing gown was seeing off a restless youth, who was hastily accepting a blessing along with a bag of money. In the second, the young man's dissolute conduct was depicted in vivid colours; he was sitting at a table surrounded by his false friends and loose women. Further on, the ruined youth, dressed in rags and a three-cornered hat, was tending pigs and sharing their food; his face exuded deep sorrow and repentance. The last one showed him returning to his father; the kindly old man, still wearing the same nightcap and dressing gown, was running out to welcome him home, while the prodigal son went down on his knees, and, in the background, the cook was killing the fatted calf and the elder brother was asking the servants what had caused all the rejoicing. Under each picture I read uplifting verses written in German. All this has stayed in my memory right up to the present day, along with the pots of balsam and the bed behind its coloured curtain, and the other bits and pieces that surrounded me at that time. I can still see the old chap himself, as clear as if it were yesterday—a man of about fifty, fresh-faced and full of bonhomie, in his long, green coat sporting three medals on faded ribbons.

I had only just finished settling my bill with the station-master when Dunya came back with the samovar. Little flirt that she was, it took no more than a second glance for her to register the impression that she had made on me. She lowered her big blue eyes. I engaged her in conversa-tion, and she responded to me without a trace of shyness, like a girl who had been out in society. I offered her father a glass of punch, gave Dunya a cup of tea, and the three of us were soon chatting away like old friends.

The horses had been ready for some time, but I didn't feel like saying goodbye to the stationmaster and his daughter. Eventually I did take my leave. The old man wished me a safe journey and his daughter came out with me as far as my cart. On the porch I stopped and asked her for a kiss. Dunya said yes. I have enjoyed a good number of kisses

Since the day I took up the trade

but none of them has left me with a longer or lovelier memory than this.

Several years went by, and circumstances brought me along the same route, to the same places. I remembered the old stationmaster's daughter, and I was looking forward to seeing her again. But, I thought, the old stationmaster might have been moved on, and Dunya was probably married by now. It crossed my mind that one or other of them might have died, and I approached the station at —— with sad forebodings. The horses were left standing by the postmaster's little lodge. I went inside, and immediately recognized the pictures depicting the Prodigal Son; the table and the bed were still in the same places, but there were no flowers at the windows, and everything around me spoke of dilapidation and neglect. The stationmaster was asleep under a thick coat; awakened by my arrival, he half-rose. It was indeed Samson Vyrin, but how much older he looked! As he busied himself copying down the details of my warrant, I took note of his grey hair, the deep lines on his unshaven face, and his bent back—and I couldn't imagine how three or four years could have transformed such a cheerful person into a decrepit old man.

"Don't you recognize me?" I asked him. "You and I are old friends."

"Might well be," he answered moodily. "This is a big road. Lots of travellers has been past here."

"What about your Dunya? Is she well?" I went on.

The old man scowled. "God alone knows."

"She's married, then?" I said.

The old man pretended he hadn't heard my question; he went on looking through my papers, whispering as he read. I stopped asking questions, and told him to put the samovar on. Curiosity was beginning to trouble me, and I was hoping that a drop of punch might loosen my old friend's tongue.

I wasn't mistaken. The old man didn't turn his nose up at the proffered glass. I began to see that the rum had cleared away his foul temper. By the second glass he was in the mood for conversation. He now remembered me, or pretended to, and I heard from his lips a story that I found both intriguing and deeply moving.

"So, you knew my Dunya!" he began. "Who didn't know her? Oh, Dunya, Dunya! What a little miss she was! Whoever came by here, they all praised her; nobody ran her down. Ladies used to give her handkerchiefs or earrings. The gents used to hang on here deliberately, like they was having their lunch or dinner, but really all they wanted was to see a bit more of her. Many a fine gentleman, no matter how angry he'd been, would calm down at the sight of her, and talk nicely to me. Believe me, sir, your couriers, your special messengers would chat with her half an hour at a time. She held the house together. Cleaning, cooking, she was good at everything. And me, like an old fool, I couldn't take my eyes off her, couldn't have been happier with her. Didn't I love my Dunya? Didn't I coddle my little baby enough? Didn't I give her a good life? No, you can't swear your way out of trouble. You can't run away from fate."

At this point he began to tell me all the grievous details. One winter night, three years ago, when the stationmaster was ruling new lines in his register, and Dunya was making a dress for herself behind the partition, a troika turned up, and a traveller in a Circassian cap and a military greatcoat, with a scarf round his neck, came in demanding fresh horses. All the horses were out. On receipt of this news the traveller was about to raise his voice along with his whip, but Dunya, who was no stranger to scenes like this, ran out from behind the partition and directed the sweetest of questions at the visitor: would he care to have a bite to eat? Dunya's appearance had its usual effect. The visitor's anger subsided, he was happy to wait for his horses, and he ordered dinner. Removing his shaggy, wet hat, unwinding his scarf and casting aside his greatcoat, the traveller revealed himself as a slim young hussar with a little black moustache. He settled down with the postmaster and struck up an enjoyable conversation with him and his daughter. Dinner was served. Meanwhile, the horses had arrived, and the stationmaster immediately ordered them to be harnessed to the traveller's covered sleigh without being fed, but, when he went back inside, he found the young man almost unconscious and sprawling across the counter. He felt sick, he had a bad headache, and he couldn't possibly drive on... What was to be done? The stationmaster gave him his own bed, and it was decided that, if the patient wasn't any better the next day, they would send to S—— for a doctor.

Next day the hussar was worse. His man rode off to S—— to fetch the doctor. Dunya wrapped a handkerchief soaked in vinegar round his head, and sat by his bed with her sewing. When the stationmaster was there the sick man groaned a good deal and said virtually nothing, though he did manage to drink two cups of coffee, and in between moans he ordered some lunch. Dunya never left his side. Not a minute went by without him asking for something to drink, and Dunya would bring him some lemonade made by her own hands. The sick man would wet his lips, and each time, as he returned the jug, he expressed his gratitude by squeezing her hand with his feeble fingers. The doctor arrived at lunchtime. He took the patient's pulse, spoke to him in German and then announced in Russian that he needed rest and should be able to resume his journey in a couple of days. The hussar handed him twenty-five roubles for the consultation, and invited him to stay for lunch. The doctor agreed. Both of them enjoyed their meal, drank a bottle of wine, and parted on the best of terms.

Another day went past, and the hussar recovered completely. He was in high spirits and he went on and on, joking first with Dunya then the stationmaster. He whistled tunes, chatted with the other travellers, wrote down their details in the post-book, and he won over the good-natured stationmaster to such an extent that on the third morning it was no easy matter for him to take leave of such a nice visitor… It was a Sunday. Dunya was dressed for Mass. The hussar's sleigh was brought round for him. He said goodbye to the stationmaster, rewarding him generously for his bed and board. He said goodbye to Dunya, and took it upon himself to drop her off at the church at the end of the village. Dunya stood there, looking undecided… "What are you worried about?" said her father. "His Honour's not a wolf. He's not going to eat you. Go on, have a lift as far as the church." Dunya got into the sleigh next to the hussar, his servant jumped up onto the box next to the driver, who gave a whistle, and the horses were off.

The miserable stationmaster could never understand why he had personally given permission for his Dunya to ride off with the hussar, how he could have been so blind, and what had happened to his powers of reason. Before half an hour had passed he felt a deep aching in his heart, and he felt so worried that he couldn't wait any longer. He went to Mass himself. As he reached the church he could see that the congregation was dispersing and there was no Dunya, not in the churchyard, and not in the porch. He rushed into the church. The priest was coming away from the altar, and a sexton was snuffing the candles. Two old women were still praying in one corner. But Dunya was not in the church. The poor parent decided to ask the sexton whether she had been at Mass. The sexton said that she had not. The stationmaster went back home more dead than alive. He had one hope left. Perhaps Dunya, like a giddy young thing, had suddenly thought of riding on to the next station, where her godmother lived. In an agony of despair he waited for the return of the troika in which he had dispatched her. The driver was in no hurry to get back. When he did finally return it was late afternoon, and he was drunk and alone. The news was mortally wounding: "Dunya went on from the station with the hussar."

This disaster was unbearable for the stationmaster. He took to his bed, the same bed on which the young crook had been lying only yesterday. Now the stationmaster, reviewing all the circumstances, could only guess that the whole illness had been a charade. The poor chap fell ill himself with a raging fever. He was taken to S——, and someone else was sent in to take his place. The same doctor who had treated the hussar was now looking after him. He assured the stationmaster that the young man had been perfectly well, and he had had an inkling of the man's evil intentions all along, but he kept quiet because he feared the whip. Whether the German's story was true, or whether he simply wanted to make a show of his clever foresight, either way it was of no consolation to the wretched patient. Even before he had shaken off his

67

illness he asked the postmaster at S—— for two months' leave, and, without telling anybody about his intentions, he set off on foot to look for his daughter. He knew from the register that Minsky was an army captain travelling from Smolensk to Petersburg. The driver who had taken him told them that Dunya had been in tears throughout the journey, though she did not seem to be travelling against her will. "Perchance," thought the stationmaster, "I shall bring home my little lost sheep." With this thought in mind he arrived in Petersburg, and he put up in the Izmaylovsky regimental barracks, at the home of a retired non-commissioned officer, an old comrade-in-arms, and there he began his enquiries. It did not take him long to find out that Captain Minsky was in Petersburg, living at the Demouth Hotel. The stationmaster decided to pay him a visit.

He arrived in Minsky's reception room first thing in the morning, asking for His Honour to be informed that an old soldier wished to see him. The orderly, busy cleaning a boot on its tree, announced that his master was still in bed, and received nobody before eleven in the morning. The stationmaster went away and came back at the appointed hour. Minsky came out to see him in person, wearing his dressing gown and a bright-red fez.

"Yes, my friend, what can I do for you?" he asked.

The old man's heart was seething, tears welled up in his eyes, and all he could say, in a trembling voice, was, "Yo... Your Honour... please will you do me a

68

favour, in God's name?" Minsky took one quick look at him, flushed red, took him by the arm and led him into his study, where he shut the door behind them. "Your Honour!" the old man went on. "No use crying over spilt milk, but still, give me back my poor Dunya. That's the least you can do. You've had your pleasure. Don't ruin her, for nothing at all."

"What's done cannot be undone," said the young man, acutely embarrassed. "I've done you wrong, and I'm pleased to ask your forgiveness, but you mustn't think that I could give Dunya up. She's going to be happy, I give you my word. What do you need her for? She is in love with me, and she's outgrown her former state. Neither you nor she could ever forget what has happened." Then, pushing something up his sleeve, he opened the door, and the stationmaster, without knowing what had happened to him, found himself out on the street.

He stood there for some time without moving. Then at last he noticed a wad of paper on the inside of his cuff; he took it out and unfolded a number of fifty-rouble banknotes. The tears came to his eyes again—tears of indignation! He crushed the notes into a ball, threw them down on the ground, crushed them with his heel, and walked away. After taking only a few steps, he stopped and thought... and went back... but the notes had gone. A well-dressed young man, catching sight of him, ran over to a driver, dived into his cab, and shouted, "Drive on!..." The stationmaster didn't chase after him. He had decided to take himself back home to the station, but before doing so he wanted to catch one last glimpse of his poor Dunya. With this in mind he came back to Minsky's house a couple of days later, but the orderly was intransigent, saying that his master was not receiving anyone. He shoved him out of the ante-room, chest to chest, and banged the door shut in his face. The stationmaster stood there for a few moments—and then walked away.

That same day, during the evening, he was walking along Liteynaya Street, coming home from a service at the Church of All the Afflicted. Suddenly a rather stylish open carriage flashed past him, and the stationmaster recognized Minsky. The carriage pulled up at a three-storey building, right outside the main entrance, and the hussar ran up the steps. A happy thought dawned on the stationmaster. He turned back, drew level with the driver and spoke to him. "Who does that horse belong to, my friend?" he asked. "Is it Minsky's?"

"Yes, it is," answered the driver. "Why do you want to know?"

"Well, it's like this. Your master told me to take a note to his Dunya, and I can't quite remember where Dunya lives."

"She lives here, on the second floor. But you're late with your note, brother. By now he'll be up there with her."

"It doesn't matter," the stationmaster retorted, feeling an inexplicable thrill in his heart. "Thank you for putting me right. I'll do what I have to do anyway."

The big door was closed. He rang, and spent a few seconds waiting in trepidation. A key turned noisily, and the door was opened for him. "Does Avdotya Samsonovna reside here?"

"Yes, she does," answered the young maidservant. "What is your business with her?"

The stationmaster walked through into the hall without giving her an answer.

"No, don't! You can't!…" the maidservant called after him. "Avdotya Samsonovna has company."

But the stationmaster, instead of listening to her, walked on. The first two rooms were in darkness; the lights were on in the third one. He walked up to the open door, and stopped. Inside the magnificently furnished room Minsky was sitting in his chair, thinking. Dunya, nicely attired to the last word in fashion, was seated on the arm of his chair like an English lady riding side-saddle. She was looking fondly at Minsky, winding his black curls round her glittering fingers. Oh, the poor stationmaster! He had never seen his daughter looking so beautiful; he could not help but admire her.

"Who's that?" she asked without looking up.

He still didn't speak. Not hearing a reply, Dunya did look up… and she cried out as she fell to the carpet. Minsky panicked and rushed to pick her up, but when he caught sight of the old stationmaster standing in the doorway, he left Dunya and came up to him, trembling with rage.

"What do you want?" he said through gritted teeth. "Why do you keep hounding me like a thief? Or are you planning to murder me? Get out of here!" And, seizing the old man by his collar with a strong arm, he pushed him out onto the stairs.

The old man went back to his lodgings. His friend advised him to file a complaint, but the stationmaster thought things over, dismissed the idea with a wave of his hand, and decided to withdraw. Two days later he left Petersburg and went back home to his station, where he resumed his old duties.

"There you are, nearly three years I've been living here without Dunya, and never a word of her. God alone knows whether she's dead or alive. Anything could have happened. She wouldn't be the first girl, or the last, to be seduced by a rake passing through, kept for a while and then dropped. There's no shortage of silly young things in Petersburg, all dolled up in satin and velvet today, but you watch—tomorrow you'll see them sweeping the streets with the riff-raff from the drinking houses. Makes you wonder—what if Dunya's going downhill like that? I knows it's a sin, but you can't help wishing her into her grave…"

This was the story as told by my friend, the old station-master, a story frequently interrupted by tears, which he wiped away with the hem of his coat, like a figure in a painting or like the passionate Terentich in Dmitriyev's beautiful ballad. These same tears were also partly induced by the rum punch, five glasses of which he put away in the course of his narrative. Not that that mattered; they still went straight to my heart. Long after we parted I couldn't forget the old stationmaster, and I kept on thinking about his poor Dunya...

More recently, as I was passing through the little town of ——, my old friend came to mind. I discovered that the station that he had been in charge of was no more. When I asked whether the stationmaster was still alive, no one could give me a proper answer. I decided to pay a visit to that familiar region, so I hired some private horses, and set off for the village of N.

This happened in the autumn. Greyish clouds covered the sky, a cold wind blew from the harvested fields, stripping red and yellow leaves from trees that stood in the way. I got to the village at sunset, and stopped at the old post house. A fat peasant woman came out onto the porch (where poor Dunya had once given me a kiss), and answered my questions by telling me that the old stationmaster had died about a year ago, the house had been turned into a brewery, and she was the brewer's wife. I began to regret my needless journey, and the seven wasted roubles.

"What did he die from?" I asked the brewer's wife.

"Drank himself to death, sir," she replied.

"And where is he buried?"

"Just outside the village, next to his late wife."

"Could anyone take me to his grave?"

"Why not? Hey, Vanya! Stop messing around with that cat. Take this gentleman to the cemetery, and show him the stationmaster's grave."

At these words a little boy with red hair, blind in one eye and dressed in rags, ran out to meet me, and soon led me out of the village.

"Did you know the dead man?" I asked him on the way.

"Oh, yes, I knew him all right. Taught me how to cut whistles, he did. When he came out of the pothouse, God rest his soul, sometimes we would go, 'Hey, granddad! Give us a few nuts!' And he did, you know. Always had time for us, he did."

"And do the travellers remember him?"

"There isn't many travellers nowadays. Magistrate turns up now and then, but he's not bothered about dead people. There was that lady what came by last summer—she was asking about the old stationmaster, and she went to see his grave."

"What lady was that?" I asked out of curiosity.

"Very nice-looking lady," the boy replied. "She was in a carriage with six horses, and she 'ad three little 'uns and a nurse with her, and a little black dog. And when they told her the old stationmaster was dead she started crying, and she said to the children, 'Sit here and be good. I'm just going to the cemetery.' I said I'd take her, but she said, 'I knows the way,' and she give me five kopecks in silver. Such a nice lady!…"

We arrived at the cemetery, a bare place, open to the elements, with a scattering of wooden crosses and not a single tree to give any shade. Never in my life had I seen a cemetery as bleak as this.

"This is the old stationmaster's grave," the boy told me, jumping up onto a sandy hillock where a black cross bearing a brass icon had been dug in.

"And is this where the lady came?" I asked.

"Yes it is," answered little Vanya. "I watched her from a long way off. She laid herself down, and she stayed there laying down for ages. And then the lady went back to the village, and she asked for the priest and she gave him some money, and then she went away, but she gave me five kopecks in silver. Wonderful lady!"

And when I also gave the lad five kopecks, I was no longer regretting the journey or the seven roubles I had spent on it.

EXTRACT FROM THE BLANK-VERSE TRAGEDY *BORIS GODUNOV* (SCENE V)

Pimen's Monologue

1603. A Cell in the Monastery of the Miracle. Night.
FATHER PIMEN, *a monk, writing under a lamp.*

PIMEN.   One record more remains, the last of all,
And then this chronicle of mine is finished,
The duty is fulfilled which God has laid
On me, a sinner. Of these many years
The Lord has made me witness not in vain,
And taught me the intelligence of books.
In days to come some persevering monk
Will come across my patient, nameless work.
As I have done, so will he light his lamp
And shake the dust of ages from these words,
And then transcribe the veritable records.
Thus shall the future sons of Orthodoxy
Learn the old fortunes of their native land,

And call to mind their great tsars, well-remembered
For all their labours, glories and good works—
While for their sins and for their darkest deeds
Before the Saviour making supplication…
Now in old age I live my life anew,
As bygone years proceed before my eyes.
Are they so long departed, filled with action
And agitated like the ocean seas?
Now they remain unspeaking and at peace.
Few faces now my memory retains,
Few words survive to call upon my ear.
The rest has gone irrevocably by…
But day is near. My lamp is burning low.
One record more remains, the last of all.

He writes.

MOZART AND SALIERI

Scene I

A room

SALIERI.   They say there is no justice on the earth.
But there is none in heaven either. This
Is clear to me, like a C major scale.
From birth I've always had a love of art;
Whenever as a child I heard the organ
Sing loud and lofty in our ancient church,
I lingered, lost in listening, until tears
Flowed from me sweetly and unbidden.
When young, I turned from frivolous amusement,
And anything unmusical I cast off
As loathsome, wrong, to be repudiated
With harsh and scornful pride. I gave myself
Only to music. The first steps were hard;
The path was wearisome. Somehow I weathered
The earliest adversities. Trade-training
I saw as the foundation-stone of art,
And made myself a tradesman, to my fingers

Imparting flat, compliant fluency
And sense of sound. I butchered sounds themselves,
Dissecting music like a corpse, believing
In algebraic harmony, and *then*,
Experienced in scientific method,
I dared to dabble in creative dreams…
And I created music—on the quiet,
In secret, with—as yet—no thoughts of fame.
And often, sitting in my silent cell
For days on end, heedless of sleep and food,
After a taste of blissful inspiration
I burned my works and watched with cold detachment
As thoughts and forms that I had given birth to
Flared up and disappeared in fleeting fumes.
What am I saying? When the mighty Gluck
Appeared, and showed us all his new-found secrets
(His so profound and captivating secrets),
Did I not give up all my former knowledge,
Which I had loved with such intensity,
To follow in his footsteps happily
And uncomplainingly, like a lost rambler
Put on the right road by a passing stranger?
By patience and intensive application
I found at last in the vast pantheon
Of art a station on the heights. For Fame
Had smiled on me; and people's hearts
Beat with my works in friendly harmony.
In happiness I quietly enjoyed

My work, my triumph, and my fame—and also
The works and the successes of my friends,
My comrades in the wondrous world of art.
No! Never did I feel the pangs of envy,
Not once! Not even when Piccini managed
To charm all those barbaric ears in Paris,
Not even when my ears heard for the first time
The opening strains of *Iphigenia*.
And who shall call Salieri's pride in question,
Describing him as someone mean and jealous,
A serpent trodden underfoot, alive
But biting sand and dust in impotence?
No one! But now—these are *my* words—today,
I'm riddled with the deepest jealousy,
Excruciating envy! Lord above!
Where is the justice when a gift from heaven—
Immortal genius—brings no reward
For burning love or selfless application,
Hard toil, devotion, hours spent in prayer,
But puts a halo on the stupid head
Of such an idle crackpot? Mozart, Mozart!

Enter MOZART.

MOZART. Ah! You have seen me. I had only wanted
    To please you with a small surprise, a joke.
SALIERI. You're here? When did you…?
MOZART.   Just now. I was bringing
    A little something that I had to show you,

But, walking past the tavern, suddenly
I heard a violin… No, friend Salieri,
You never in your life heard anything
So funny… A blind man inside the tavern,
Playing *Voi che sapete*. Wonderful!
I couldn't help it. I have brought the fiddler
To entertain your good self with his art.
Come in!..

Enter a blind old man holding a violin.

Please will you play a bit of Mozart?

The old man plays an aria from Don Giovanni. MOZART
chuckles.

SALIERI. And do you find this funny?
MOZART.   Oh, Salieri!
Surely you think it's funny, too?
SALIERI.   I don't.
It isn't funny when a wretched dauber
Shows me a smear of Raphael's *Madonna*,
It isn't funny when a dreadful poet
Dishonours Dante with some parody.
Get out, old man.
MOZART. Wait. Here's a little something.
Drink to my health.

The old man walks off.

Salieri, I can see

You're out of sorts today. I'll come again
Some other time.

SALIERI.   What have you brought to show me?

MOZART. It's nothing special. No. The other night
I found I couldn't get to sleep as usual,
And two or three motifs occurred to me.
I wrote them down this morning, and I wanted
To hear what you might think of them, but now
Is not the right time for you…

SALIERI.   Mozart, Mozart!
There's no wrong time for you. Oh, please sit down.
I'm all ears.

MOZART (*at the piano*). Well, imagine someone… Who?
It could be me… let's say a younger version,
Someone in love—a little, not too much.
I'm with a nice girl, or a friend… like you…
I'm happy… Then—a vision of the grave,
A sudden darkness comes, or some such thing.
Listen to this.

He plays.

SALIERI.   You came here, bringing *that*,
And you could call in at a drinking den
Because of some blind fiddler! God in heaven!
Mozart, you are not worthy of yourself.

MOZART. Is it all right then?

SALIERI.   Oh, the depth of feeling!
The bold inventiveness and elegance!

82

You, Mozart, are a god, and you don't know it.
I do. I know.

MOZART.　　　Go on! You mean it? Hmm…
But anyway, my godliness needs feeding.

SALIERI. Listen, why don't we go and dine together?
Let's try the Golden Lion.

MOZART.　　　　　Very good.
That's fine by me. But let me slip back home.
I need to tell my wife not to expect me
For supper.

Exits

SALIERI.　　　I'll be waiting. Do not fail me…
No! This is it. I cannot any more
Defy my destiny. I have been chosen
To stop this man. If I do not, we perish,
We priests and all who serve the cause of music—
Not me alone, my hollow reputation…
What good will come from Mozart living longer
And rising, as he will do, to new heights?
Will he uplift the cause of art? No, no.
For art will fall again when he is gone.
He will not leave us any good succession.
What use is he? He's like some Cherub, who
Comes down to us, and brings celestial songs,
Filling us sons of dust with wingless longing,
Only to leave the earth and fly away.
Well, fly away, then! Better now than later.

83

Here's poison, my Isora's parting gift.
I've kept it by me all these eighteen years,
And in that time my life has often seemed
Like a deep wound while I have sat at table,
Facing an unsuspecting enemy,
And never once have I capitulated
To whispering temptation, even though
I am no coward, and I've been humiliated,
And have no love of life. I bide my time,
Despite my agonizing thirst for death.
Why should *I* die? I thought perhaps one day
Life might endow me with unhoped-for gifts;
I could perhaps be visited one night
By blissful ecstasy and inspiration.
Perhaps great art would be created
By Haydn, born again to my delight…
How I enjoyed a hated guest at table,
Thinking perhaps that one day I should find
A foe far worse; perhaps the vilest slight
Would fall upon me from a sniggering height—
And then Isora's gift would serve me well.
And I was right! At last I have discovered
My enemy, and Haydn, born again,
Has filled me full of wondrous ecstasy.
The time is now! O sacred gift of love,
This day be plunged into the cup of friendship!

Scene II

An inn. A private room with a piano. Mozart and Salieri seated at a table.

SALIERI. Why are you out of sorts today?

MOZART.   I'm not.

SALIERI. Well, really, Mozart, you do seem upset.
    The food is good, the wine is wonderful,
    So why the silence? Why the frown?

MOZART.   It's true,

    I am upset… My requiem…

SALIERI.   Oho!

    When did you start to write a requiem?

MOZART. Some time ago. Three weeks or so. It's weird…
    Surely I must have told you?

SALIERI.   No.

MOZART.   Well, listen…

    Two or three weeks ago I came home late
    One evening. I was told someone had called
    To see me. I could not imagine why.
    All night I wondered who this man could be.
    What did he want of me? He came again
    The next day, but he didn't catch me in.
    But on the third day I was on the floor,
    Playing with my young boy when I was called.
    I went to see. There stood a man in black,
    Who bowed low, placed an order with me for

A requiem, and walked out. I sat down
And set about composing. Since that day
My man in black has never called again.
I'm glad of that. I do not feel like parting
With my new work, the requiem, although
It is now finished. In the meantime…

SALIERI. Yes?

MOZART. I feel embarrassed to admit it…

SALIERI. What?

MOZART. By day or night I cannot rest from him,
My man in black. He's with me everywhere,
Chasing me like a shadow. Even now
He's with us two in a triumvirate
At table.

SALIERI. Say no more. These childish worries…
Forget this empty thinking. Beaumarchais
Has often said to me, "Look, friend Salieri,
Whenever dark thoughts rise and come upon you,
Go and uncork a bottle of champagne
Or read through Mozart's *Figaro* again."

MOZART. Oh, yes, that Beaumarchais, a friend of yours—
He was the man for whom you wrote *Tarare*,
A splendid piece. It has one melody…
That I remember well on happy days…
De-dum, de-dee… Oh, is it true, Salieri,
That Beaumarchais once poisoned somebody?

SALIERI. I don't think so. That man had too much humour
To trade in things like that.

MOZART.   He is a genius,
    Like you and me. And genius and evil
    Are incompatible. Don't you agree?
SALIERI.   You think so?

Drops poison in Mozart's drink

                    Have a drink then.
MOZART.   Your good health,
    My friend. Here's to our honest partnership,
    The bond that holds us—Mozart and Salieri,
    Two sons of harmony together.

Drinks

SALIERI.   Wait!
    Wait, wait! You've drunk! Couldn't you wait for me?
MOZART (*throwing his napkin down on the table*).
    That's it. I'm full.

Goes over to the piano

                    Listen to this, Salieri.
    My requiem!

Plays

                You're weeping?
SALIERI.   Tears like these,
    Unshed before, are made of pain and pleasure.
    It feels like having done a heavy duty,
    It feels as if a healing knife has severed
    A limb that was diseased! These tears, dear Mozart...

Ignore them, please. Keep playing, move on quickly
To fill my spirit overfull with sounds…
MOZART. If only everyone could feel the power
Of harmony, like you. But no. The world
Could not exist if that were so. Nobody
Would bother with the squalid cares of life,
And all would wallow lavishly in art.
We chosen men are few, we happy idlers
Who disregard base functions of the day,
We priests of nothing but the beautiful…
Is it not true?…
                    But I'm not feeling well…
A heavy pain inside… I'll have a sleep…
I'll say goodnight.
SALIERI.   Goodnight.

Alone

                              You'll go to sleep,
Mozart, for a long time… But is he right?
Perhaps I'm not a genius. Maybe genius
Is incompatible with evil. No!
Take Michelangelo… Or was that story
Dreamt up by hoi polloi? The Vatican
May *not* have been created by a killer!

                                        1825

THE BRONZE HORSEMAN

Foreword

The occurrence described in this story is based on real events. Details of the flood are taken from contemporary journals. Anyone interested may consult the report by V.N. Berkh.

Introduction

Gazing across a watery waste,
He of the mighty visions faced
The farthest deeps. Vast in its scope,
The river carried, as it raced,
One miserable little boat.
The swampy banks were mossy green
With dark huts few and far between,
The homes of lowly Finnish folk.
The forests, through their misty screen,
Where hidden sunbeams never broke,
Murmured with noises.

And he pondered:
"We'll scare the Swedes away. This place
Shall see a city strongly founded,
Flung in our brazen neighbour's face.
A window into Europe we
Shall cut by Nature's own decree,
And build a solid sea-shore station.
Borne here across the unknown main,
All vessels we shall entertain.
And freely spread our celebration."

A century saw the city's birth,
A lovely wonder of the north,
From darkest woods and swampy earth
Magnificently rising forth.
Where Finnish fishermen before,
Stepsons of Nature, all alone,
Stood sadly on the shallow shore
And cast into the depths unknown
Their rotting nets—in this place now
Along the living banks see how
Huge, shapely buildings throng and rise,
Tower and palace: vessels race
In fleets from earth's remotest place
To quaysides rich with all supplies.
The Neva now was clad in stone.
New bridges crossed the water, while,

Dark, decorating every isle,
Green were the gardens which had grown.
The capital, of younger life,
Outshone the Moscow that had been,
As an ascendant ruler's wife
Outshines the purpled, widowed queen.

O Peter's work, I love you so!
I love your stateliness and strength,
The Neva's soft, majestic flow,
The granite bordering her length,
Your iron railings' hard design,
And through the thoughtfulness of night
Your limpid twilight's moonless shine.
When in my room I stay to write
Or sit, without a lamp, to read,
The sleeping streets shine clear indeed,
Vast masses emptied of their people;
Bright, too, the Admiralty steeple.
The darkness is denied possession
Of this, the golden firmament.
Dawn follows dawn in swift succession;
Night's borrowed half-hour is soon spent.
I love your cruel winter, too,
The still air and the frosty shiver,
Girls' cheeks with more than rosy hue,
The sledging down the Neva river,

The brilliance, noise and talk there is
At balls; the single fellow's turn
To feast, when glasses foam and fizz,
And in the punch the blue flames burn.
I love, in lively, warlike duty,
Cadets upon the Martian field,
Foot soldiers, cavalry, revealed
In level and unchanging beauty,
The rippling, orderly array
Of banners torn, victorious ones,
Their helmets, wrought in shining bronze,
Shot through by bullets in the fray.
I love you, capital of Mars,
When fortress cannons smoke and roar
To welcome to the house of tsars
A son, the northern queen's gift, or
To greet new victories in war
And raise triumphant Russian voices,
Or when the Neva starts the motion
Of cracked blue ice towards the ocean
And, with a sense of spring, rejoices.

O Peter's town, like Russia, here
Stand splendidly and firmly founded!
Peace with the elements is near,
The elements which you confounded.
The wrath and chains of yesteryear

May Finland's waters soon forget,
Nor with their futile rage upset
Tsar Peter's everlasting sleep.

A time of dread there was. We keep
A memory of it not yet old…
And of these times, my reader friend.
The story shall I now unfold
From sorry start to grievous end.

Part One

On Petrograd the dark mists rose,
November blew and autumn froze.
The noisy Neva splashed ahead
And in her shapely confines heaved,
As does a sick man, in his bed
Tossing and turning, unrelieved.
And in the midnight darkness rain
Beat bitterly upon the pane.
The keening tempest howled and squalled.
After a visit homeward came
A youth. Yevgeny was his name.
Our present hero shall be called
By such a title, since its sound
Delights the ear: my pen has found

Before a friendly air about it.
His surname? We can do without it,
Though years ago it might have been
In something of a bright position,
And in the hands of Karamzin
A great sound in our land's tradition;
And yet the world and tongues of men
Do not recall it now as then.
Somewhere our hero is employed,
The great he chooses to avoid,
Lives in Kolomna, never weeping
For ages lost or kinsfolk sleeping.
Yevgeny, then, arriving home,
Took off his overcoat, undressed,
Lay down, but couldn't sleep or rest,
So widely did his wild thoughts roam.
What did he think about? That he
Was poor; that honest toil might see
Him grow to be of good repute
And of the self-sufficient kind;
That God might further contribute
To fill his pocket and his mind;
That many a lucky man displays
A lack of wit and lazy ways
And yet lives easy and secure!
That he had worked two years together.
He also thought about the weather,
Relentless still; by now, for sure,

From off the river, as it lifted,
The Neva bridges had been shifted.
He and Parasha some few days
Would walk in separated ways.
Yevgeny gave a heartfelt sigh,
And set off dreaming like a poet:

"Marriage? Why should I never know it?
Life would be hard, of course, but I,
With youth and health, am well prepared
To labour night and day, unspared,
And I shall find a way to build
A humble shelter, plain to see,
Where all Parasha's cares are stilled.
And in a year or two, maybe,
I'll get a little job and give
Parasha care of where we live
And also of the children: thus
We shall live, and, hand in hand,
Together till the grave we'll stand.
Our grandchildren shall bury us…"

Thus did he dream that night, alone
In sadness. If the wind and rain
Would only ease their plaintive moan
And not attack the window pane
With such a fury…

          Heavy-eyed,
At last he slept. The stormy grey
Fades from the misty night outside,
And thins before a pale new day...
A day of horror!
            All that night
The Neva faced both storm and sea,
Crushed by their wild stupidity,
Until she could no longer fight...

By morning crowds were teeming by
Along her banks to watch and wonder
At waters splashing mountains high
And foaming furiously asunder.
But gales were blowing from the bay
To block the Neva; coming round,
She stormed and seethed, and in her way
The islands, one by one, were drowned.
The weather raged with greater force,
The Neva, rising in her course,
A roaring cauldron, swirled and spat,
Then, like a savage beast, leapt at
The city... All that stood before
Recoiled and ran. The space around
Soon stood deserted. Underground,
The cellars filled before the spate,
Canals gushed up at every grate.

Petropolis was soon to be
Waist-deep, like Triton, in the sea...

A siege! The wicked waters strike,
Climbing through windows, burglar-like.
The stems of boats in full career
Smash panes. Now hawkers' trays appear
With covers soaked; beams, roofs go past
From broken huts; cheap things amassed
By poor, pale beggars, few by few;
Storm-shattered bridges; coffins, too,
From steeping cemeteries exhumed,
Swim down the streets!..
                  The people fear
God's wrath and sense his judgement near.
Their food, their shelter, all is doomed!
Where shall they turn?
                  In that dread year
The glorious Tsar, now at his rest,
Ruled Russia still. Then out came he,
Sad, stricken, on the balcony.
"The Tsars," he said, "may not contest
God's elements." In deep remorse
He sat and watched, with pensive air,
Disaster take its evil course.
A lake had formed in every square,
With great, wide torrents rushing there

Down all the streets. The palace lay,
A sorry island now. The Tsar
Spoke out; and, hurrying away
To thoroughfares both near and far,
His generals went up and down
In peril from the storming tide
To save the people, terrified
And waiting in their homes to drown.

And at this time in Peter's square
A great new corner-house stood, where,
Paw raised, each like a living cat,
Above the elevated entry,
A pair of lions stood on sentry.
Astride one marble beast here sat,
Arms folded and without his hat,
Yevgeny, still and deathly white,
A wretched figure, filled with fright
—Not for his own sake. And although
A wave rose hungrily below,
Lapping the very shoes he wore,
Though winds began to howl and blow,
And lashed his face with rain, and tore
His hat away… he did not know.
His eyes were brimming with despair,
Fixed rigid on one place to keep
A constant watch. Like mountains, there,

Arising from the angry deep,
The raging waters towered high,
The tempest howled there, sweeping by
With wreckage. Lord! There by the bay,
A stone's throw (alas! no more) away
From the water's edge, he seems to see
A plain fence and a willow tree,
A little house in poor repair.
Parasha, whom he dreams of seeing,
Lives with her widowed mother there…
…Or has he dreamt them into being?
Is all life empty, merely worth
A dream where heaven mocks the earth?

And he, as if he were enchanted,
As if the marble held him planted,
Cannot climb down! At every quarter
Lies an unbroken stretch of water,
And with its back towards him, why,
Above the Neva's stormy course,
Rearing implacably on high,
One arm outflung across the sky,
The Idol straddles his bronze horse.

Part Two

At length destruction was to pall
And then—the taste of fury cloying—
The Neva stole away, enjoying
Her very insolence and gall,
Indifferently letting fall
Her loot behind. In this way, too,
A robber with his vicious crew
Bursts on a village, sacking, routing,
Cutting, smashing, to screams and shouting;
Teeth-gritting clashes, frightened faces
And savage frenzy… Piled with loot
And fearing possible pursuit.
The weary vandal homeward chases
And strews his plunder down the street.

The roadway, on the waves' retreat,
Lies open. My Yevgeny races,
His spirits sinking, bittersweet
With fear and hope, till he draws near
The torrent's half-subdued career.
But, filled with their victorious thrill,
The waters seethed with evil still,
As if a fire lay deep-concealed.
The Neva, foam-flecked in her course,

Breathed heavily like some great horse
Galloping from the battlefield.
Yevgeny looks, a boat he spies,
And runs up to this lucky prize,
Hailing the ferryman, and he,
Who ferries on without a care,
Agrees for only a modest fare
To row him through the fearsome sea.
With stormy wave on stormy wave
Long did the expert oar contend;
Through them the crew, however brave,
Risked constantly a plunging grave
In such a craft, till… in the end
It reached the shore.

                       He rushes through
A well-known street to well-known places,
Not recognizing what he faces,
Wretched before the awesome view,
With everything in disarray
And all torn down or swept away.
Some cottages stand all awry,
Some are in ruins, others lie
Demolished by the waves. All round
The scene is like a battleground,
With bodies strewn to left and right.
Yevgeny, failing in his mind,
Weak from his agonizing plight,
Runs straight to where he is to find

The hidden news, known but to Fate,
As in a letter sealed up fast.
Down through the suburb quickly... wait,
Here is the bay, the house just past...
What's this?...

        He stopped dead in his track,
Retraced a step or two, came back.
He stares... moves on... another stare...
Shouldn't the house be standing there?
Here is the willow, but the gate...
Swept off . . . The house cannot be found!
With darkest cares to contemplate,
He walks in circles, round and round,
Only to rend the air and rave.
Then, beating on his brow, he gave
A sudden laugh.

        Night's mist came down
And settled on the trembling town.
But late the people stayed awake,
Gossiping, wondering what to make
Of that past day.

        The rays of morn
From storm clouds pallid now, and worn,
On a peaceful capital shone through.
The troubles of the day before
Had left no trace. A purple hue
Held the evil hidden and ignored.
The former order was restored.

Down streets where freedom had returned
Walked people coldly unconcerned,
Their shelter of the night forsaken.
Clerks left for work. Bold and unshaken,
The huckster opened up again
His cellar, pillaged by the flood,
Aiming to make his losses good
With profits made from other men.
And boats were lifted from the yard.
Already Count Khvostov, the bard
Beloved by heaven, immortal master,
Was versifying the disaster
With which the Neva's banks were scarred.
My poor Yevgeny, wretched figure...
Alas! His mind was so hard pressed
It could not stand the awful rigour
Of all these shocks. The wild unrest
Of Neva and the tempest's sound
Rang in his ears. Silent, obsessed
With dreadful thoughts, he roamed around.
Some dream tormented his mind's eye.
Although a week, a month went by
They never saw him homeward-bound.
His empty, cosy room was hired
The day the landlord's time expired,
To some poor poet. His things neglected
Yevgeny never came to claim.
A stranger, by the world rejected,

All day he wandered without aim,
Sleeping on quays; for food he found
Odd morsels on some window sill.
He wore the same poor clothing still,
All torn and rotting. At his back
Stone-throwing hooligans would play.
The coachman's whip would often crack
And lash him as he made his way,
A figure on the highroad, blind,
Oblivious to all around,
It seemed, and deafened by the sound
Of terrors ringing in his mind,
Thus dragging out his sorry span,
Akin to neither beast nor man,
Not anything, not earthly stuff,
Not lifeless spirit…

               Once, he slept
Down by the Neva dockside. Rough
Breathed out the wind, as summer crept
To autumn. Sombre billows leapt
And foamed and moaned upon the docks
On velvet steps, like one who knocks
At judges' doors to press his case,
Ignored by them in every place.
He woke, poor creature, to the dark
And drizzle; a sad wind howled, and hark!
The watchman's cry out yonder might
Be an echo called across the night…

Yevgeny gave a start. Appalled
By horrors vividly recalled,
He leapt up, set off roaming, then
Quite suddenly he stopped again,
And slowly looked around and cowered,
His face distorted wild with fear.
A mansion house above him towered,
A great big house with columns. Here,
Raising a paw, above the entry,
Lifelike, the lions stood on sentry,
And in the darkness, high indeed
Above the rock and railing, why,
One arm outflung across the sky.
The Idol straddled his bronze steed.

Yevgeny shuddered. Horribly clear
His thoughts had grown. For now he knew
This place the floods had sported through,
Where grasping waves had crowded near,
All round, rebellious and grim,
Those lions, and the square, and Him,
Towering high, unmoving. He,
Whose bronze head crowned the darkness still,
Had founded by his fateful will
This city by the very sea…
Fearsome in all the darkness now!
What contemplation in that brow!

What strength and sinew in him hidden!
And in that horse what fiery speed!
Where do you gallop, haughty steed?
Where will those falling hooves be ridden?
O mighty overlord of fate!
With iron curb, on high, like this,
Did you not raise on the abyss
Our Russia to her rampant state?

This poor, demented creature here
Went walking round the Idol's base:
His wild eyes sought and found the face
Of him who ruled a hemisphere.
He felt a tightness in his breast.
Against the chilly railing pressed
His brow. His misted eyes were staring.
He felt a boiling in his blood,
A blazing in his heart. He stood
Before the proud colossus, glaring,
With gritted teeth and fingers crushed.
Like one with evil powers filled;
"You, and the miracles you build!"
He hissed, and shook, angrily flushed,
"I'll have you…" Then away he rushed
Headlong, all of a sudden discerning
The dreaded Tsar—or so he thought—
In a flash of mounting fury caught,

And softly, slowly, his face was turning…
And out across the empty square
He runs; behind him, he would swear,
A crashing roll of thunder moves,
Of ringing and resounding hooves
Upon the quaking thoroughfare.
And, splendid in the pale moonlight,
One arm flung out on high, full speed,
Comes the Bronze Horseman in his flight,
Upon his crashing, clanging steed.
The poor mad creature! All that night,
No matter where his footsteps led,
Still the Bronze Horseman in his flight
Leapt on behind with heavy tread.

From that time on, when chance directed
That he should walk the square again,
Uneasiness would be reflected
Upon his face. Hurriedly, then,
A hand upon his heart he pressed
To still the torture in his breast.
His tattered, shabby cap was doffed;
Eyes worried, never raised aloft,
He edged along.
                        An islet stands
Close by the shore. Late at his trade,
Sometimes a fisherman, delayed,

Comes with his fishing net and lands
To cook his frugal supper. Or
Some office worker comes ashore
Upon the island-waste, out rowing
On Sunday. Not a single blade
Of grass has grown there. Freely flowing,
The floods washed up here, as they played,
A mean old shack. There it survived,
A black bush darkening the deep.
One day last spring a barge arrived
And took it off, a ruined heap,
Deserted. Near the door they found
My madman. As the Lord ordains,
They gathered up his cold remains
And there they laid them in the ground.

1833

TSAR NIKITA AND HIS
FORTY DAUGHTERS

Once there lived a tsar, Nikita—
No one's life was ever sweeter.
He was neither good nor bad;
Oh, what happy lands he had!
Duty's path he duly trod,
Eating, drinking, serving God.

Tsar Nikita's wives aplenty
Bore him daughters two times twenty;
Lovely, charming girls all forty,
Angels all—not one was naughty—
Forty darlings pure and sweet,
Each with, oh, so lovely feet,
Raven tresses of the choicest,
Gorgeous eyes and gorgeous voices.
Were they silly girls? Oh, no!
Every one from top to toe
Was a captivating creature,
Perfect—*but for one lost feature*.

One lost feature? What was that?
Nothing to be wondered at,
Nothing much—a bit of nonsense—
Though it was still lost in one sense.
I'll explain as best I can,
Though I must not cross that man,
(Pious idiot of idiots),
Mr Censor, so fastidious.
"Give me words, Lord," here one begs…

Well…
        These girls…
                Between their legs…

Not so fast!…
        It's no good rushing;
Modesty's already blushing.
Start again, good taste protests.

Well… Take Venus. Oh, the breasts!
Oh, the lips, the feet! I love them,
But the thing I love above them,
What I really long to touch…
Is… Well what? Oh, nothing much,
Nothing, just that bit of nonsense…
This was what was missing long since
From the young princesses, yes,
In their lively impishness.

Wondrous was their birth; reaction
Ranged from outright stupefaction
In the hearts of all at court
To their father, left distraught,
And their mothers, sadly chastened.
Naturally the midwives hastened
To the people with the news.
Jaws dropped, issuing aahs and oohs
In amazement. Ever after,
Anyone who felt like laughter
Stifled it. For suchlike tricks
They could send you to the sticks.

Tsar Nikita called his courtiers
With the maids who served his daughters,
And he gave this stern decree:
"Just let any one of ye
Show my girls the least transgression,
Give them any thinking lesson,
Or so much as hint at what
My princesses have not got,
Or on double meanings linger,
Or make rude signs with your finger,
Then from woman shall be wrung—
Mark my words—her dirty tongue,
But from *man*—expect no pardon—
That which has been known to harden."

Tsar Nikita, strict but fair,
Spoke his clear word. Everywhere
People kowtowed at this earful,
Careful from now on, and fearful.
No one's ears could now lie slack;
Everybody watched his back.
Every wife, herself a dumb thing,
Feared her husband might say something
While the husbands thought, no doubt,
"Let my wife blurt something out!"
(All the men were pretty furious.)

So the girls grew up, incurious,
Poor things… Royal councillors
Heard the Tsar, behind closed doors,
Tell the story of the sisters
Hugger-mugger, all in whispers,
So the servants couldn't hear.

They considered the affliction:
What could make it disappear?
Then, with a quick genuflection,
One old councillor drew near,
Touched his bald pate reverently
And said rather hesitantly,
"O wise Tsar! Your slave am I.
Please forgive me the presumption
If I speak of the vile function
Of my body in years gone by.

Once I knew a skilled procuress
(Does she somewhere still endure as
A provider? Maybe yes!)
She was deemed a sorceress
Who could cure ills and distempers,
Even raising flagging members.
This witch should be found somehow.
She can cure things. She will listen.
She'll install whatever's missing."

"Go and find this woman, *now*!"
Loudly thundered Tsar Nikita.
"Find this woman!" he repeated,
Furrowing an angry brow.
"But beware. If she starts cheating,
If she fails in what we're seeking,
If she fools us, even *tries*,
If we catch her out in lies,
I'm no tsar if I don't one day,
On the first day after Sunday,
Burn the woman at the stake!
This I say for heaven's sake."

They were secret, they were cautious,
But on royal postal horses
Messengers were sent to scan
Every corner of the land,
Riding, probing every cranny.
Would they find the magic granny?

One year passed, then two—no word,
Nothing seen and nothing heard.

Then, at last, one of these fellows
Found a warm trail. Young and zealous,
Deep into dark woods he went
(Clearly by the devil sent).
Lo! A cottage in a clearing—
Yes, the witch's! Nothing fearing,
He, the Tsar's own appointee,
Went straight in—and there stood she.

Boldly did he bow and greet her,
Then he told of Tsar Nikita
And his daughters, and what not—
What it was they hadn't got.
She, with just a little snigger,
Packed him off with witchy vigour,
Saying, "Take yourself away,
Don't look back and run off quickly
Or a pox will make you sickly.
Come back three days from today
For a parcel and a warning,
And come in the early morning."

Then the witch, away she stole,
Locked her door and stocked up coal.
Three days passed… Her magic revel
Summoned up the very devil

With a little casket, brought
For transmission to the court,
Full of bits of sinful "hership"
Which we fawn upon and worship,
Every type—all good ones too—
Every size and shape and hue,
Curly-wurly—Lord have mercy!

Having sorted them, the witch
Counted forty beauties, which
She then wrapped in cloth, and passed it,
Locked inside the devil's casket,
To the waiting journeyman,
With his silver. Off he ran.

On and on he goes, till sundown,
When he stops, fatigued and run-down.
He must have a nibble first,
Then some vodka for his thirst.
(He was well prepared, meticulous—
Go without? Don't be ridiculous!)
He unbridled his good steed,
Settling nicely down to feed.
There's the grazing horse; just past it,
He sits dreaming of new ranks:
Count or Prince? (Nikita's thanks.)

What is that inside the casket?
What goes thus from witch to Tsar?

Well, he squints in through the keyhole.
Nothing. Damn the locked-up wee hole!

Oh, how brave the curious are;
Curiosity runs riot,
So he listens… All is quiet
In the box. He gives a sniff.
"Something there. I know that whiff!
The suspense—I can't abide it!
Shall I have a look inside it?
All these tensions, let them loose!"

So, he raised the lid, and—whoosh!
Feathered birdies, fluttering dancers,
Swarmed up onto nearby branches,
Perching, with tail feathers prancing.

Hey! Our envoy tempts them back.
Eat my biscuits—have a snack!
Little crumbs he vainly scatters.
(Their taste runs to different food!)
Loud they sing—that's all that matters.
Caskets, prisons—they're no good!

Here a bent old crone came strolling
Down the road with heavy tread,
On her stick. Our envoy said,
"Save me! I shall lose my head!
Help me, please. I need you, mother.

Look, I'm in a spot of bother.
I can't catch them. Help! Relief!
How can I assuage this grief?"

She looked at him, gave a croak,
Spat upon the ground, and spoke.
"Yes, your action was degrading,
But all is not lost. Weep not.
Simply show them... *what you've got*,
And they won't need much persuading."
"Thank you very much," he said,
Showing all... From overhead
With no hint of hesitation
Birdies flew down to their station.

Lest there be yet more mischance,
Any risk of something naughty,
Now he locked them up, all forty,
And set off for home at once.

The princesses, of all ages,
Put their gifts away in cages.

From all sadness now released,
Tsar Nikita gave a feast.
Days and nights they feasted seven,
One month resting, as in heaven.
He made all the Council rich,
And did not forget the witch.

From his curio collection
He sent her a nice selection:
Magic wax in spirit (which
All admired), two asps entangled
And two skeletons that dangled.
Yes, our envoy got his gold…

And my story now is told…

Now I can expect suggestions.
Stupid comments. Silly questions.

Why this nonsense?… Why the joke?…

I like speaking, and I spoke.

1822

EXTRACT FROM
YEVGENY ONEGIN

This brief extract comes from Chapter Four, about halfway through the novel.

Tatyana Larina has fallen for the superficial charms of Yevgeny Onegin, and written to him. He has now turned up in person to give his response. Instead of taking advantage of her, he has advised her to be more cautious, and admitted that he would never make a proper husband. Pushkin now reflects on his behaviour, praising him for letting the young girl down lightly, but imagining that his enemies (some of whom are also his friends) will not be as charitable. This provokes negative thoughts on families and friends, and a cynical conclusion that the only person you can trust is yourself.

ANTHONY BRIGGS

17

Thus, like a preacher, spoke Yevgeny.
Eyes blinded, as the salt tears choked,
Tatyana, breathless, uncomplaining,
Was listening to him as he spoke.
He gave his arm. Far from ecstatic,
With movements now called "automatic",
She leant on him (nothing was said),
And languidly inclined her head.
They came back round the kitchen garden,
Strolling together. No one would
Have thought this anything but good,
For rural laxity can pardon
Most things, within its happy laws,
As also snooty Moscow does.

18

Reader, you must be in agreement:
Poor Tanya was gently let down.
Nothing but good was all that *he* meant.
Yevgeny once again has shown
That his pure soul could not be deeper,
And yet the ill will of bad people

Has spared him nothing, though his foes
Along with so-called friends, yes those
(Friends, foes—the difference may be worthless),
Pay him some desultory respect.
Foes flourish; but, to be correct,
From *friends*, not foes, may God preserve us.
Friends, friends of mine—they give me pause.
I recollect them with good cause.

19

Why so? Well, it is my intention
To put some blank, black dreams to sleep,
And *in parenthesis* to mention
That there's no jibe too low or cheap,
Spawned by a gabbler in a garret
For high-born scum to hear and parrot,
No phrase too gross for any man,
No vulgar gutter epigram
That won't be smilingly repeated
In front of nice folk by your *friend*
"In error", for no wicked end,
Though endlessly acclaimed and greeted.
But he's still friends through thick or thin
Because he loves you—you're akin.

20

Ho hum. I ask you, noble reader,
How are your people? Are they well?
Permit me to insist you need a
Pointer from me so you can tell
What is the point of *family members*.
Families have their own agendas;
We must indulge them, show them love,
Woo them in spirit like a dove,
And, following the common custom,
See them at Christmas, and, at most,
Send them a greeting through the post,
And then we can relax and trust 'em
To disregard us through the year...
God grant them long life and good cheer.

21

But still, the love of gorgeous ladies
Outweighs the claims of friends and kin;
With this—whate'er the storms from Hades—
You're in control, *you* rein things in.
Oh, yes, despite the whirl of fashion,
And nature with her wayward passion,

And world opinion… all that stuff…
But the sweet sex is light as fluff.
Besides, a husband's fixed opinions
Must be observed throughout her life
By any truly virtuous wife.
Thus one of your female companions
Can suddenly be swept away.
Satan loves love. Watch him at play.

22

Who shall be loved? Who can be trusted?
With whom do we risk no betrayal?
Who weighs our words and deeds, adjusted
Obligingly to our own scale?
Who never blackens us with slander?
Who's there to coddle us and pander?
Who sees our sins as "not too bad"?
Who will not bore us, drive us mad?
Stop your vain search for lost illusions:
You're wasting all your strength and health.
The one to love is *you yourself.*
You are, good reader, in conclusion,
A worthy subject, we insist,
For no one kindlier exists…

THE PROPHET

Dragged on by my sick, yearning soul,
I roamed the dark night of the desert,
And found a crossroads, where—behold!—
I faced a glorious, six-winged seraph.
He touched me, dreamlike, feather-fingered.
Upon my very eyes he lingered;
They shone, like a shocked eaglet's, wide,
Prophetically revivified.
He touched my ears, into them pouring
A ringing and a mighty roaring.
I heard the shuddering heavens speak,
And angels soaring in the vault,
And sea-beasts squirming in the salt,
And in the valleys vines that creaked.
He touched my mouth and from it wrung
My sinfully back-biting tongue,
Full of deceit, and he inserted
With fingers dripping yet with blood
Into my palsied mouth for good
The sting and wisdom of a serpent.

And with his sword he clove my breast
And tore out from the bleeding hole
My throbbing heart, and into it pressed
Another heart of burning coal.

I lay like death where I had trod,
And hearkened to the voice of God:

Prophet, arise and follow me,
Seeing and hearing, saith the Lord.
Go forth upon the land and sea
And burn hearts with the living Word!

1826

TO ANNA KERN

I still remember all the wonder,
The glorious thrill of meeting you,
The momentary spell of splendour,
Spirit of beauty pure and true.

When sadness came upon me, endless,
In vain society's direst days,
I heard your voice, your accents tender,
And dreamt of heaven in your face.

Years passed, with stormy days diffusing
My young dreams into empty space,
And I forgot your voice's music
And heaven's beauty in your face.

Then, far from home, in exile, chastened,
I watched the weary days go by.
No tears for me, no inspiration,
No sense of God, no love, no life.

You came again. My soul remembered
The glorious thrill of meeting you,
The momentary spell of splendour,
Spirit of beauty pure and true.

Now once again my heart is racing,
Proclaiming the renewal of
My former tears, my inspiration,
My sense of God, and life, and love.

1825

WINTER EVENING

Darkness falling, stormy roaring,
Whipping winds and scurrying snow.
Baying beasts are howling for me,
Babies wailing—blow, winds, blow!
Through the tattered rooftops, flapping,
Rustling through the threadbare thatch,
Like a late-night traveller tapping,
Rattling at the window latch.

Here inside your little cottage
All is sadness, all is gloom.
Dear old lady, you say nothing
By the window of our room.
Are you weary of the windy
Blows and buffets that we feel,
Or the whirring of the spindle
And the whizzing of the wheel?

Here's to you, my dear old nanny,
Good companion of sad years.
Here's to grief—there isn't any!
Drink with me the cup that cheers.

Tell me tales again, old lady.
Sing to me again your rhymes:
Tales of tomtits, and of maidens,
Tales of once upon a time.

Darkness falling, stormy roaring,
Whipping winds and scurrying snow.
Baying beasts are howling for me.
Babies wailing—blow, winds, blow!
Here's to you, my dear old nanny,
Good companion of sad years.
Here's to grief—there isn't any!
Drink with me the cup that cheers!

1825

THE UPAS TREE

In parched and barren desert land,
Where blazing sunshine sears the earth,
The Upas Tree, a grim guard, stands
Alone in all the universe.

Nature one day on that dry plain
Begot it in a surge of wrath,
Piercing the dead green leaves to stain
Its boughs and roots with a poisoned broth.

Now poison oozes through the bark,
Melting at high noon, to become
Hard and stiff in the evening dark,
Glassy coagulated gum.

No bird, no tiger dare approach.
Only black whirlwinds on occasion
Visit this pestilential growth,
And speed off with their vile contagion.

And if a roving cloud should chance
To moisten its thick leafy strands,
From every newly poisoned branch
Dark poison laves the burning sands.

But one man sent another man
To the Upas Tree, by order stern.
Obediently away he ran,
And with the poison soon returned.

He brought the deadly gum. The bough
And its fine foliage were withered.
Suddenly down his pallid brow
Cold streams of perspiration slithered.

He brought the gum and lay down, weak,
On the tent matting. Moments later
The poor slave perished at the feet
Of the implacable dictator,

Who soaked his slavish arrowheads
In poison sure to overwhelm,
Disseminating with them death
To humankind in every realm.

1828

MAN FOUND DROWNED

Children looking for their father
Rushed into the house and said,
"Daddy, Daddy, we've been fishing,
And we've caught a man. He's dead!"
"Fishing? Little devils. *Fibbing!*"
Father growled and tore his hair.
"Kids again! You little buggers,
Fishing corpses? Don't you dare!

That would mean the law, and questions…
All them words. They move so slow!…
Come on, wife, there's nothing for it,
Where's my coat? I'd better go…
Where's this body?" "Down there, Daddy."
And it's true. The father gawps.
By the creek, near the spread netting,
On the sand there is… a corpse.

Ghastly body, slimy, swollen,
Blue all over, hideous skin.
Could it be some poor old dosser
Topped himself in all his sin?
Or a fisherman who fell in,
Or a lad who drank too much?
Or a dealer caught by muggers,
Who they thought was a soft touch?

"I'm a farmhand. Not my problem.
Look round quick. No one about.
Get the body in the water,
Grab the legs and shove it out."
And he heaved it from the steep bank,
Shoving outwards with a stave,
And the dead man flowed downriver
Searching for a cross and grave.

Yes, the dead man in the water
Floated, bobbing on the foam
Like a bloke that was still living.
Farmhand watched him and went home.
"Follow me, you little puppies,
And you'll get a little treat.
Only—not a word to anyone,
Or I'll knock you off your feet."

Then that night the weather worsened
And the river boiled up black,
And the kindled splinter dwindled
In the farmhand's smoky shack.
Children sleeping, wife a-slumber,
Farmhand lies on his high box.
Through the howling storm he listens.
At the window… someone knocks.

"Who's that knocking?" "Let me in, boss."
"Why, what's wrong with you out there?
Are you Cain, and am I Abel?
Devil sent you. I don't care.
I don't want no trouble from you.
Here it's cosy, nice and warm."
Still, he opens up the window,
Slowly moving hand and arm.

Storm clouds stir… A stream of moonlight…
Ugh! A naked man appears,
Eyes like saucers, wide and staring,
Water streaming from his beard,
With his body, numb and lifeless,
Arms a-dangle, dribs and drabs,
And his bluey, bloated body
Black with bristling, clinging crabs.

But the farmhand slammed the window
When he knew his naked guest.
"Get lost, damn you!" Wild, he whispered,
Terror-stricken and distressed.
All night long he raved with horror,
And he shivered in a state
At the numbing all-night knocking
On the glass and at the gate.

Now the people tell the story
Of a man who every year
Waits, a miserable farmhand,
For a weird guest to appear.
Morning, and the weather worsens,
Storms blow when the night is late,
And a drowned man comes a-knocking
On the glass and at the gate.

1828

'WINTER. WHAT SHALL WE DO?'

Winter. What shall we do out in the country? I greet
My servant as he brings my morning cup of tea
With questions. Is it cold outside? Has it stopped
           snowing?
Is there a covering? Should I perhaps get going,
Go for a ride—or stay in bed all day and labour
Through these old magazines passed on by a
          kind neighbour?
There is fresh snow, so up we get, and we're away—
A muffled clip-clop trot; the light of early day.
Wielding our riding crops, off with the dogs we fly
To search the pale snow with a scrutinizing eye.
We wheel across the countryside, till late we roam,
Then—two missed hares behind us—suddenly
          we're home.

Oh, what a life! As night falls, to the blizzard's howl,
The candle gutters, and my heart shrinks. All is foul.
I drink the boredom down, slow poison, drop by drop.

Let me try reading. No, the letters blur… I stop.
My thoughts have wandered miles away… The book
                                                    snaps shut.
I sit down, seize the pen, cajoling my muse, but
She is too sleepy. All her words have lost their hold.
The sounds won't come together. I have no control
Over my handmaid, Rhyme, strange girl. My words
                                                    go wrong.
My cold and misty lines drag their slow length along.

I weary of my lyre, with both of us so fractious.
Out in the drawing room, what topics now distract us?
The sugar-works and the municipal election…
My hostess apes the weather in sourness of complexion.
Her speedy, steely needles clack, and then she starts
A little fortune-telling with the king of hearts.

Oh, aching boredom! How the days drag,
                                                    far from town!

But, if, in this sad hamlet, as the night comes down,
When I sit playing draughts, tucked quietly away,
Perhaps there should arrive a carriage, or a sleigh,
Bringing chance visitors thrown suddenly amidst us,
A mother and her girls (two blonde and shapely sisters!),
Then how the backwoods stir—what life this visit brings!
The world, because of it, brims over with good things!

The eyes meet first in angled, lingering observation,
And then a word or two leads on to conversation,
Warm laughter and an evening singing with the sisters,
With whirling waltzes, secret dinner-table whispers,
Long, languid glances mixed with bantering repartee.
Protracted meetings on the close stairs, she with me…

Onto the twilit balcony at last she sneaks,
Her neck, her bosom bared, the snowstorm at her cheeks.
But northern storms can never harm a Russian rose!
Her warm kiss sears the frosty night, her ardour glows.

O lovely Russian girl, snow-silvered and so cool!…

1829

'WHEN I STROLL DOWN A BUSY STREET'

When I stroll down a busy street,
Or linger in a crowded church,
Or if wild youth and I should meet—
I let my idle dreams emerge.

I tell myself: the world keeps turning.
However many of us are here,
We're all bound for the vaults eternal,
And someone's hour is always near.

A lone oak tree attracts my gaze.
I think: this patriarch sublime
Will long outlive these empty days,
As it outlived my father's time.

When I caress a little child
I think: farewell, I've had my day.
You take my place, I'm reconciled —
Yours is to thrive, mine to decay.

I always say goodbye in thought
Each day, each year, and try to guess
Which day in which year will have brought
The anniversary of my death.

Where is my death? Where is my doom?
In battle? Far afield? At sea?
Or will perhaps some nearby combe
Encompass what remains of me?

Although the senseless human frame
Cares not at all where it should moulder,
I'd like to end up, all the same,
Near places that I once thought golden.

And at the entrance to my tomb
May young life frolic dissolutely.
And may impassive Nature bloom,
Shining with everlasting beauty.

1829

140

'OH, I HAVE LOVED YOU'

Oh, I have loved you, and perhaps my spirit
Still harbours a warm glow of love today.
But God forbid that you be burdened with it;
I would not sadden you in any way.

I loved you in a wordless, hopeless fashion,
Sometimes in jealous rage, sometimes struck dumb.
I loved you with a deep and tender passion.
May you be loved like this in years to come.

1829

'NO, NOT FOR ME THE STORMIEST PLEASURES OF THE SENSES'

No, not for me the stormiest pleasures of the senses,
Voluptuous enjoyment, overwhelming frenzies.
No, not the groans of some Bacchante, or her cries
When, squirming like a snake, in my embrace she lies,
Hurrying me along, eager to know what bliss is,
And shuddering to her crisis in a storm of kisses.
No, you're much lovelier than this, my gentle lamb.
How agonizingly happy with you I am
When you have said you won't, and now you say you will,
Only to yield yourself with no delight or thrill,
Cold to my protestations and exuberance,
Restrained in sympathy and lukewarm in response,
Until I feel you melt, in your reluctant fashion,
Coming to me at last and sharing in my passion.

1830

142

'WHEN I REACH OVER TO ENFOLD YOU'

When I reach over to enfold you,
Encompassing your slender form
And ever breathing, as I hold you,
Transports of love to keep you warm,
You slither from me silently
With such a lithe and lively rhythm;
Then, darling, you respond to me
With a sharp smile of scepticism.
Determined never to forget
A sad tradition of betrayal,
Unsympathetic and upset,
You scarcely heed my lover's tale…
I curse the ventures mean and shady
Of distant days when youth ran riot,
Waiting in gardens for young ladies,
All anxious in the evening quiet.
I curse love's whispering in the ears,
The magic melody of verse,
The easy girls, and, what is worse,
Their late misgivings and their tears…

1830

'THE TIME HAS COME,
DEAR FRIEND'

The time has come, dear friend. My heart now longs
                                                    for peace.
The days are flying by, and each hour, as it flees,
Subtracts a tiny part of life. Though you and I
Make plans for life together—all too soon we die.

There is no happiness, but there is peace and freedom.
I have been dreaming of an enviable Eden—
Weary of slavery, long have I planned my flight
To a distant home of work and innocent delight.

(late poem, undated)

AUTUMN

(A FRAGMENT)

What does not at this time enter my drowsing mind?

Derzhavin

1

October's here again. The trees will soon have tossed
The last leaves down from their bare branches. Now

the chill
Of autumn breathes on us. The road is hard with frost.
Although the stream still courses, babbling past the mill,
The pond is frozen over. Galloping across
The open fields, my neighbour tastes again the thrill
Of chasing: fine the sport, and bruised the winter wheat.
His baying hounds arouse the woodlands from their sleep.

2

This is the time for me! Springtime I can't abide,
With all that smelly, thawing slush. My spirits yearn.
My blood seethes, my heart aches and I feel ill inside.
I'm altogether happier with winter stern.
I love the snowy waste, the sleigh, the moonlit ride
So fast and free, when you sit cuddling your girl.
Her face is warm and fresh, her sable glistens black.
You squeeze her hand, she squeezes passionately back.

3

Oh, for the bladed boots! How good to pull them on
Down by the solid river, and skate upon the glass!
And what about the games, that special winter fun?…
Yes, but… Snow follows snow till half a year has passed.
And, long before that, even Bruin, the shaggy one,
Grows weary in his lair. You get fed up at last
Of sleighing with the sirens ever and again,
Or moping by the stove and at the window pane.

4

Summer! I might have loved you like a precious jewel,
But for the stifling heat, the dust, the gnats, the flies.
You desiccate the mind, your days are long and cruel.
We suffer with the arid landscape as it dies.
We are obsessed with drinking, finding something cool,
And soon we think of Mistress Winter's sad demise.
We packed her off with wine and pancakes. Very nice.
But now we call her back with ice-cream treats and ice.

5

The closing days of autumn are often not held dear,
But this is just the time by which I am beguiled.
It glows with modesty; its beauty is austere.
In Nature's family I love the unloved child.
To be quite frank, this is the only time of year
To which I am by nature fully reconciled.
There is much good in it. I love it with sound reason.
I am aware of something special in this season.

6

How can this be explained? Autumn appeals to me
In the same way as a young consumptive girl might
Appeal to you. Condemned to death, poor creature, she
Fades uncomplainingly towards the gathering night.
Upon her pallid lips a playful smile you see.
The yawning grave is there, but still beyond her sight.
Her lovely face is delicately lilac-shot.
Today she is alive, tomorrow she is not.

7

Season of sadness! Now my eyes imbibe the splendour
With which you decorate the year as it grows old.
I love the countryside in all its fading grandeur,
The thinning of the woods, the purple and the gold,
Blown treetops whispering in voices soft and tender,
The leaden heavens where the rising mists have rolled,
The sudden sunbeams and the frost of early morning,
When greybeard Winter sends his first long-distance
                                                                                    warning.

8

In autumn every year I come into full flower.
The thrilling Russian cold inspires me
                                                    through and through.
I love my life again each day and every hour.
My appetite returns on time, and sleep does, too.
My blood is up, my glad heart surges with new power.
Desire and joy are mine, I'm young, the world is new,
Fresh life wells up in me… Such is my constitution.
(If you'll forgive such a prosaical intrusion.)

9

They bring my horse round. Mettlesome, he shakes
                                                    his mane
And gallops off with me to range the open spaces.
The frozen valley now rings to a new refrain
Of clattering hoofs and cracking ice, as on he races.
But soon the short day fades and we are home again.
Too long neglected, now how warm the fireplace is!
Flames flare and fall. I read, and soon begin to ponder,
Letting my unrestrained imagination wander.

10

And I forget the world… The sweetness and the quiet
Lull all the feelings of my waking mind to rest.
Poetry comes to me: I am awakened by it.
Here is the lyric power, my spirit is possessed,
I tremble inwardly, magical sounds run riot.
My dreamt imaginings struggle to be expressed,
And visitors unseen swarm over me at last,
Figments of my fancy and people from my past.

11

Many the bold ideas that swim into my ken
And instantly meet rhymes to match them sweet and true.
The pen calls for the hand, the page demands the pen.
Poetry then pours forth in lines of every hue.
Thus may a galleon stand, becalmed and sleeping, when
Suddenly comes the call! At which the scrambling crew
Swarms up and down to spread the swelling canvas wide.
The giant sallies forth, cleaving the surging tide…

12

Where are we bound?…

1833

ELEGY

The dead delights of frenzied younger days
Weigh on me like an alcoholic haze.
The aching sadness of my past endures,
And, like good wine, gains body as it matures.
My future life is grim—without relief,
A surging swell of struggle, toil and grief.

And yet, my friends, I have no wish to die:
I want to suffer, live and wonder why.
I know I can expect—amid the torment,
Trouble and care—the rare, delicious moment.
Sweet harmonies will fill me with delight,
And I shall weep with joy for what I write.
And it may be that at my sad demise
A smile of love will shine in someone's eyes.

1830

REMEMBRANCE

When for us mortal men the noisy day is stilled,
    Hushing the city squares as they
Settle in limpid twilight, languidly distilled,
    And sleep rewards the toil of day,
My hours, unsleeping in interminable silence,
    Draw out their long, tormenting course.
In the blank night I feel with ever-sharper violence
    The serpent's sting of my remorse.
Imagination seethes, my mind is fraught with anguish.
    Swarming with dark ideas untold,
Before my eyes remembrance speaks its silent language,
    Disclosed on an uncoiling scroll.
Reading the ghastly story of my bygone days,
    I shudder, cursing, all-despising,
Burning with bitter tears—yet I shall not erase
    One line, however agonizing.

1828

'I HAVE MY MONUMENT'

Exegi monumentum.

The Roman poet Horace started his final ode with the now famous line "*Exegi monumentum aere perennius*" ("I have raised a monument more durable than bronze").

Pushkin's imitative tribute, more formal than most of his other work, is a similar assertion of confidence that his reputation as a writer will endure.

ANTHONY BRIGGS

I have my monument, not built by human hands.
Well-trodden is the path to it that men will follow.
Indomitable it has raised its head, which stands
    Higher than Alexander's Column.

Not all of me will die, for in my lyric strains
My spirit shall endure; the grave shall not destroy it.
I shall be famous still while ever there remains
    Under the moon a single poet.

Word of me shall go out through all the lands of Rus,
Where each and every people shall pronounce

                              my name—
That grandson of the Slavs, the Finn, the wild Tungus,
    And the Kalmyk out on the plain.

Long will the people love my name, and for

                              good reason:
That I was one who roused kind feelings by my verses.
That in a cruel age I sang the cause of freedom,
    And for the fallen called for mercy.

Hearken, O Muse, to what is ordered in God's name:
Ignore all calumny and ask no crown or jewels.
Receive with equanimity both praise and blame.
    Do this—and have no truck with fools.

                            21st August 1836

THE BOOK OF PARADISE
ITZIK MANGER

THE ALLURE OF CHANEL
PAUL MORAND

SWANN IN LOVE
MARCEL PROUST

THE EVENINGS
GERARD REVE